BOOTS

BOOTS

Running from Poverty and God

DAVID FORD

WESTBOW
PRESS®
A DIVISION OF THOMAS NELSON
& ZONDERVAN

WestBow Press books may be ordered through booksellers or by contacting:

WestBow Press
A Division of Thomas Nelson & Zondervan
1663 Liberty Drive
Bloomington, IN 47403
www.westbowpress.com
1 (866) 928-1240

ISBN: 978-1-9736-6632-5 (sc)
ISBN: 978-1-9736-6705-6 (hc)
ISBN: 978-1-9736-6633-2 (e)

Library of Congress Control Number: 2019908512

Print information available on the last page.

WestBow Press rev. date: 6/27/2019

To my loving mother, who made sure I was raised to attend church and love the Lord. Her life was very short here on earth, but her life in heaven will go on for eternity. If you are a Christian, I will introduce you to her someday when we get to heaven.

This is an uplifting novel featuring James, who is nicknamed Boots, as he goes from a poor child with a future in lowly paid farming to a college student with a track scholarship that opens a myriad of options. This includes living as a devout Christian, since his coach was a believer. But during his journey through life, Boots faces adversity, including driving drunk and causing a terrible accident. How will his life turn out? Readers will have to keep turning the pages to find out!

This is the story of James Harris. James lived with his parents, Jim and Louise Harris, his two older sisters, and his brother on a cotton plantation in southern Mississippi. The year was 1952.

Their house was nothing more than a shack that had been on the plantation for over a hundred years. James's grandparents had lived in it prior to his parents being married.

Jim and Louise had worked their entire lives for the owner of the plantation, "Mr. Bill" as everyone called him. His name was actually William Longhurst.

The plantation had been in Bill's family for generations. Cotton was the primary crop raised now. The farm still produced both cotton and tobacco, but cotton was the backbone of the plantation.

James's father, Jim, had once worked picking cotton, but now with his back and health conditions declining, he worked mostly in the tobacco production.

Louise had declined in health after years of bending over and picking cotton from sunrise to sunset, so she now worked mostly in Mr. Bill's plantation house, doing laundry and household chores.

The income of Jim and Louise was below the poverty level, but luckily they could live in the house rent-free and were given some land they could farm to grow most of their own food.

Even though they both believed in God, they rarely attended church. Sunday afternoon was the only time they were not working on the plantation. Louise would help prepare meals for Mr. Bill's family, and Jim would usually have things he needed to do on the farm as well.

One of the good things about Sunday meals was that Louise and the other women who helped prepare it were allowed to take any leftovers home to their families.

Both of James's parents were good people, but with the situation they were in, neither could provide much for their children but love.

James's older sisters had dropped out of school and gotten married, while his older brother, Matt, had quit and joined the army. James was finishing up eighth grade but had no ambitions of graduating high school. No one could remember anyone who had finished high school in their family for generations.

James was not very popular in school. He went to school with a lot of other poor students, but he seemed to be more of a loner.

His clothes were always hand-me-downs, and the only time he wore shoes was when he went to school.

James went to his last class of the day, which happened to be physical education. The teacher's name was Coach Richards, and he was one of James's favorite teachers. Coach Richards would often joke with James and carry on small talk, which none of the other teachers did.

James walked into the gym and sat down, while some of the students went and changed into tennis shoes and shorts. James had neither, so he participated in whatever he had on, which was usually a ragged pair of jeans, an old T-shirt, and a large pair of boots.

As the students were sitting in the stands, Coach Richards approached the group. After checking the roll, he said, "Today we are going to finish up the remainder of the school year performing a physical fitness test. I know some of you took it last year in the seventh grade, so we want to see how much you improved since then.

"This is a test of several events, including running, jumping, and strength tests to see where you rank as far as the nation goes. We will send the results to the State Department, and they will be analyzed according to your age, weight, and how you score on each event. Then they will compare it to the previous years to see how students are improving or declining as far as their physical fitness goes.

"Today we will perform the standing long jump, and tomorrow you will be timed in the hundred-yard dash. The other events you will perform are the softball throw, high jump, running long jump, and the mile run. We also have to test you on the number of pull-ups you can do, but we will do that on a day it's raining and we can't go outside. Are there any questions?"

One of the students asked if it would affect their PE grade.

"It won't lower your grade, but if someone does really well on the test and their grade is not already an A, it can help pull it up.

"Everyone, go out to the track near the long jump pit, and we will begin the standing long jump. The last one out of the gym, close the door please."

Outside, each student had three jumps, and the longest one was written down.

When James's name was called, he stepped to the starting board and started to jump.

"Wait a second, James. You can't jump with those big boots on," the coach said.

James looked down at the big boots he was wearing. The boots were actually three sizes too large, but they were all he had. He went over and sat down and pulled them off. He didn't have any socks on because he didn't have any that didn't have holes, so he never wore any.

James took his three jumps, put his boots back on, and then sat down. His longest jump was about average compared to the other boys in the class.

The following day, the class would perform the one-hundred-yard dash.

Once again, each student would perform by himself or herself, and the times would be written down.

After James heard his name called by Coach Richards, he walked to the starting line.

"Not boots again," Coach Richards said. "You can't get an accurate time in those big boots, son."

From that day on, James became known as Boots. Several years later, no one could remember his real name; he was Boots to everyone.

James took his boots off and ran the one-hundred-yard dash barefooted. It was no big deal to him since he hardly ever wore shoes at home.

When they got back to the gym and the other students were getting dressed, Coach Richards yelled at James to come to the storage room.

James walked in the door and saw all kinds of football equipment lying on big shelves.

Coach Richards said, "Let's go to the back of the room."

There were boxes full of old football cleats. "Do you know what size shoes you wear?" the coach asked.

James had no clue. All his shoes had been hand-me-downs. He had never had a real pair of shoes of his own.

Coach handed him a couple of different shoes to try on. Then he finally said, "Looks like nine and a half is what you need."

James was confused. The only running event left was the mile. Was the coach expecting him to run a mile in a pair of football cleats?"

Before he had time to ask, the bell rang. "Better go and catch your bus before you miss it," the coach said.

When he got home that night, the coach made a call to a pastor friend of his and asked if he had any size 9.5 tennis shoes in the items that had been donated to the church for redistribution.

The pastor called him back and told him he had two pairs.

The following day as gym class began, Coach Richards called James into his office. "We are going to run the mile today. I want you to wear these shoes when you run."

Coach handed him the tennis shoes, and there was a new pair of socks inside them. "Will you do that for me, Boots?" The coach laughed.

The shoes were not new, but they were the most comfortable James had ever worn. It felt like he wasn't even wearing shoes.

Instead of running one at a time, all the girls ran, and then all the boys. Coach explained the different strategies involved in running the mile. He told them not to start out too fast but to try to run a good, steady pace and then go all out on the last lap.

James had never been anybody in school. Most students just ignored him or pointed at him and snickered; today, that was about to change.

As the race began, James decided to run as if he were running by himself. He ran all over the plantation in the summer, so he didn't see any big deal about running a mile.

After the first turn, he was out in front all alone. Maybe he had gone out too fast. He remembered what the coach said, but this just seemed natural to him.

As he crossed the line for the first lap, he heard the coach yell to him to not burn himself out.

The shoes felt so light; he had never felt this good running. He didn't look back to see that he already had a forty-yard lead over the second-place runner.

The second and third laps were the same as the first; he kept increasing his lead.

The coach shook his head, knowing that at any moment he would probably see Boots fall to the side of the track in exhaustion.

As Boots started down the backstretch of his final lap, Coach saw a change in the running stride of Boots. He thought, *Just as I thought. Here goes the collapse.*

Instead, Boots ran even faster; no one was within 150 yards of him.

As he crossed the finish line, the nearest runner was 180 yards behind.

Coach Richards looked down at the stopwatch and couldn't believe it. He kept staring at the watch and almost missed the second-place runner's time. The watch read 5:20.3. This was the time a good high school senior would run.

The coach was reading the times off for one of the students to write down, but he couldn't keep his mind off of Boots's time. He thought, *What time would he have run if he had spikes and someone pushing him?*

As Boots began to walk back to the starting line, the boys started coming across to finish their race. The girls began running up to Boots and bragging on what a good runner he was. No girls had ever paid any attention to him before, except to make fun of him or put him down.

Before the class went back into the school, Coach Richards said, "It's supposed to be rainy tomorrow, so we will do the pull-ups in the gym. Before we leave, I just want to say that the run you just saw by Boots is one of the most amazing things I have ever seen in sports. His time ranks up there with your better high school seniors who run track. Three cheers for Boots."

They cheered and congratulated Boots all the way to the gym.

Boots kept thinking of how great his feet felt with a pair of shoes that actually fit.

As the bell rang to go home, the coach stopped Boots and said, "Young man, this can be your ticket out of here. You can become a great runner. It can change your life if you will dedicate yourself."

Boots didn't know what all the fuss was about; all he did was go out and run like he had done for years. His parents didn't own a car, and he didn't have a bicycle, so if he wanted to get somewhere without taking all day, he just ran.

At the supper table that night, his mother asked, as she always did, how his day at school had gone.

Boots told his mother that they had a test in spelling, and he didn't think he did very well. He wasn't sure about telling her about the race and what the coach had said, so he just told her they had to run a mile in PE class.

As they were getting up from the table, he remembered the shoes. He had left them in his locker at school. He decided to wait and bring them home to show his mother tomorrow.

Whereas Boots downplayed the day's events, his coach did the opposite. He called the high school track coach to tell him what happened. He wasn't at home, but his wife told him she would have him call when he got home.

Coach Richards couldn't wait to tell the high school coach what had happened. It was getting later and later, and still no call. He thought about calling back but decided to wait a little while longer.

Finally, the phone rang. He almost dove to pick it up.

"Hello," he said.

"Hey, Coach. This is Coach Marks. How is it going?"

"Hey, Tom. You owe me big-time." Coach Richards laughed.

"What trouble have you gotten me in this time? Seems I stay in trouble with someone all the time—not running their son in the right race, practicing to long, or not practicing long enough. You name it, I've done it."

"No, man, I'm going to make you famous. I have discovered a runner that will make you coach of the year." Coach Richards went on to explain what happened at the track that day.

"I don't have anyone on my track team right now who can run a 5:20 mile," Coach Marks replied.

"Can you imagine, with coaching, what this kid could become?" Coach Richards said.

"What kind of person is this kid?"

Coach Richards replied, "He is a quiet kid who was raised with nothing and seems to be a hard worker."

"Tell him tomorrow that I want to talk to him about coming out for high school track next year, and I'll stop by and talk to him as soon as I can," Coach Marks replied.

"I sure will. Can you imagine what time he would have if he had been wearing spikes and had someone pushing him?"

"He is only in the eighth grade and just a little over a minute over the national high school mile record now. I'll have trouble sleeping tonight." Coach Marks laughed.

Coach Richards couldn't wait for the last period to come so he could talk to Boots.

Since it was raining outside, they were to do the pull-ups portion of the test. Coach Richards had a chair pulled up beside him. He asks Boots to sit beside him and write down each person's number of pull-ups. He actually wanted to be able to talk to Boots without the other students hearing him.

Coach asked him if he had ever thought of going out for track in high school. He found out that Boots didn't know anything about track. They had no TV at home, so all he knew was people ran around in circles.

The coach explained to him that he could be a great track star in high school. He went on to tell him that he was just a little over a minute more than the national high school record. With proper training and equipment, he should be one of the best high school milers in the United States by his senior year.

"If you are, that means you can go to any college in the country and run. If you get a college education, you can become whatever you want to be and make a good salary."

"But I have to work on the plantation when I get home from school. I can't stay after school for practice," Boots replied.

Coach Richards hadn't thought of that. A lot of the poorer students had to go to work after school. Many would miss several weeks when crops were ready to be harvested.

"Coach Marks will work around that. Don't worry," the coach said. But in his mind, the coach was worried. He would need to practice—and practice hard—to get to the next level.

That night, Coach Richards called Coach Marks and told him about his conversation with Boots.

"That would be a problem; he won't get a lot better if he can't come and practice. Maybe you and I can go talk to the parents and get something worked out."

Both coaches didn't sleep much that night, trying to figure out what to do. Boots had so much potential, and this would probably be his only chance to get out of the poverty he was destined to grow up in.

The following day, Coach Richards asked Boots if he could call and talk to his parents about setting up a meeting with him and Coach Marks. He found out that they didn't have a phone and Sunday afternoon was the only time they didn't work.

Coach asked Boots if he had told his parents about how fast he had run the mile. He told him no but that he had shown his mother the shoes he had given him.

The two coaches tried to figure out what to do. Finally, Coach Marks asked where Boots lived. Coach Richards said that they lived and worked on the Longhurst plantation.

"Wait, that might be our solution. Mr. Longhurst is on the school board. If we explain the situation to him, maybe he will allow Boots's parents to have some time off to let us talk to them," Coach Marks said.

"Well, it's worth a try. All he can do is say no."

"There is a school board meeting next Thursday. I'll try to talk to him before or after the meeting and tell him what's going on," Coach Marks said.

The following Friday, Coach Richards received a call telling him that Mr. Longhurst had agreed to let the parents meet with them the next afternoon after school, since it was supposed to rain. That way, his parents wouldn't miss much work during planting time.

The meeting was set up for the following day. There were supposed to be heavy rains throughout the week. When Mr. Longhurst told Boots's parents they would be allowed off work at three the following day to attend a meeting with two of the teachers from school, they assumed that James must be in some kind of major trouble.

Later that night at the supper table, his parents asked James what he had done wrong for his teachers to ask for a meeting with them. James had no clue until he heard the names of the two teachers. He then told his parents about the race at school. His parents weren't buying that the meeting was about him running around some silly track.

The following day, the coaches met Boots and his parents on their front porch. To their surprise, Mr. Longhurst asked if he could attend the meeting.

The coaches explained the unbelievable time Boots had run and how it could be the potential for him to receive a great education, and it might lead to a well-paying job.

"We have no records, but his 5:20 mile might be a world record for an eighth grader," Coach Richards said.

"If he can knock ten seconds a year off his time, he will be a world-class miler. He will be able to go to any college in the country," Coach Marks added.

"How much money will he be paid to run?" Boots's father asked.

The two coaches looked at each other.

"He won't receive any money, but he will be able to get a good education, which will lead to him getting a good job, which will pay a lot of money," Coach Marks said.

"No one in our family has ever graduated from high school, and you're expecting us to believe that he will graduate from college?" his mother said.

"Yes, ma'am, we are. There is no reason he should not be able to," Coach Marks said.

"So, what are you asking us to do?" his father finally said.

"He needs to be able to practice and train. That means he would need to stay after school and work out."

"No way. We have a certain amount of work that needs to be done, and I'm too old to pick up his slack," his father said.

Mr. Longhurst said, "Would he have to stay after school every day?"

"Track occurs in the spring, so it would only be for a couple of months—March and April," Coach Marks said. "We usually have four or five meets on Saturdays."

"That's the months we need him the most," his father replied. "That's spring planting season."

"This would be a great opportunity for James to maybe make something of himself and get out of this hard labor, but he is right, spring planting and fall harvest are our two busiest times," Mr. Longhurst said.

Everyone just sat in silence for several minutes. Finally, Coach Richards said, "What about this. Boots—I mean James—can practice running during his PE class until track season. Then he still can practice during PE, but he can also practice with the track team one or two afternoons. When there is a track meet on Saturday, I will come and work the planting in James's place."

"Why would you do that?" asked James's mother.

"Because I believe he can be one of the best runners to ever come out of Mississippi, and I want to see him get an education and make something of himself."

"On days we don't have a track meet, I will come and help plant crops too," Coach Marks said.

"Jim, you and Louise have worked for me all your lives. You have been loyal and faithful and as hard of workers as I could ask for. He's your son, but I think he deserves this opportunity to make something of himself. I will be dead and gone then, but I hate to think that forty years from now, he will still be here having to work as hard as you two have. I say let's give him this chance to change his life," Mr. Longhurst said. "Jim, do you and Louise agree?"

Jim looked at Louise and said, "It would be nice for him not to have to work like we have all our lives. Nice to finally have someone in the family make it through high school too. I say we let him go for it."

Everyone laughed and smiled, but then Coach Richards had a thought: no one had asked Boots if this was what he wanted. How could he have been so stupid not to have even asked Boots if he wanted to run track? Maybe he didn't even want to run.

He had no clue where Boots was. He had not told him they were meeting with his parents after school.

"Is James around so we can tell him what we have decided?" the coach asked.

"He's out in the barn working. I'll go fetch him," Jim said.

Mr. Longhurst and Louise began talking, and Coach Richards motioned Coach Marks over and whispered, "What if Boots doesn't even want to run track?"

"I hadn't thought of that. We may have put the cart before the horse."

James and his father came walking back from the barn. When they got to the porch, Coach Richards explained all that they had talked about.

The moment of truth had arrived. Coach Marks asked James if he wanted to be on the track team the following year.

James smiled and said, "I sure like running a lot more than I do picking cotton. When do we start?

Everyone clapped and cheered. Now if he could just live up to everyone's expectations.

As he was driving home, Coach Richards began to think of all the things that could go wrong. What if he wasn't as good as they thought? What if his stopwatch wasn't working correctly and he wasn't that fast?

What if he got an injury and wasn't able to run? What if he wasn't the nice kid he thought he was?

Coach Marks came to Boots's school to talk to him about how to train and gave him a schedule to follow during the summer months. The problem was, in the summer, Boots had to work until dark, and he didn't have the time to train. Another problem was that he wasn't getting a healthy diet. At school, he ate what his mother packed for him. In the summer, he ate whatever was brought to him in the field—not a very nutritious meal—to provide energy.

Coach also found out Boots had no real shoes to train in. All he had was a pair of too big boots and the tennis shoes he was given at school, so he went to the store and bought him the best pair of running shoes he could afford. When he gave them to Boots, tears formed in his eyes. He put them on and said they felt like he had no shoes on; his feet were so light. Coach didn't tell him it would take him several months to pay for them; he just acted like the school had bought them.

Coach Marks tried to keep in touch with Boots as much as he could, but he always seemed to be working. Sometimes he would catch him at home on Sunday afternoons. He found that Boots was having pain in his shins from running. He advised him to take a few weeks off and not run. Track season was a long way off, and there was no use in training hard this time of year. He really didn't see how he was able to train after working from daylight until sunset. He and his body had to be exhausted, and this is when injuries occur. He tried to get Boots to run only a couple of miles a day until school started. Then he could up his workouts.

As the new school year began, Boots found out high school was a lot harder than junior high. The subjects were harder, but his counselor advised him he would need these subjects if he planned on going on to college.

Being near Coach Marks every day allowed the workouts during gym classes to be more structured. He would work on distance running some days and sprints other days. Some days were very light. He also got better meals, with Coach Marks paying for the meals at school out of his own pocket. In addition, he wasn't working all day in the field, so workouts were a lot easier.

He had not told Coach, but several times during the summer, he had decided not to run track. He was working from daylight to dark, eating, and then going out and running. He was so exhausted that he fell into bed, and it seemed like it was time to get up before he knew it. He kept telling himself if he didn't make something of himself, he would live the same life as his mother and father. He knew they would never be able to retire but would have to work until the day they died.

As the year progressed, Boots settled into a routine. As days grew shorter with winter approaching, he didn't have as much work to do when he got home, so he was getting a lot more rest. He was able to increase his mileage work, even though he had to run the dirt roads in the dark.

It took him a few months, but he was finally learning how to develop better study habits. In the spring, when daylight increased and planting was underway, he was so tired when he got home and ate he usually just fell in bed without doing any homework or studying. He wasn't sure how he was going to add running track to the spring schedule and make it through.

The first few weeks of track practice, he was able to attend about twice a week, but he knew as planting season approached, he would probably be lucky to get one practice in a week.

The first meet was coming up the following Saturday. Coach Richards had called Mr. Longhurst and told him he would be there to work in Boots's place, just like he had promised.

Boots was getting nervous. He had never run in a real track meet, nor had he ever seen one.

The big day finally arrived. Boots had been warned about running the mile. He could go out too fast or too slow, and it was not unusual for runners to try to bump their opponents off the track.

Boots was a nervous wreck; he just wanted to get it over with.

He wished his parents could attend, but he knew they would be working from daylight until dark, as normal. That was the life he was trying to get out of.

The announcement finally came for all milers to take their mark.

As he stepped to the line, he realized that everyone in the race was older than he was, and many were seasoned seniors. He just hoped he could run a smart race and not finish last.

He had never worn a uniform of any kind, and he was wearing shoes with spikes on them for the first time. He hoped he wouldn't fall flat on his face when the gun sounded.

The starter said, "Runners, take your marks, set," then the gun sounded.

Boots almost fell over the runner next to him. He regained his balance, and as they exited the first turn, he was in last place. *So much for going out too fast*, he thought. *I didn't go out fast enough.*

There was a lot of pushing and shoving that he had been warned about, but he didn't expect it to be this bad. It was like they were doing it on purpose.

Going down the backstretch, everyone seemed to settle into a rhythm. Boots though it was an awfully slow pace, but he was afraid it was just his nerves, so he stayed in last place.

As they passed the starting line, a coach was yelling out the split times. Boots now realized that the pace was too slow, so he started working his way to the front.

When they finished their second lap, Boots was in third place. He still felt like the pace was too slow. He hoped he wasn't making a big mistake, but he moved around the first two runners coming out of the second turn.

As they crossed the line finishing their third lap, Boots was ten yards ahead. Everyone was afraid he had run too fast a pace and would have nothing left for the final lap.

Boots had always started his final kick coming out of the second turn. He figured he could stand any pain for three-fourths of a lap. The problem was a lot of runners felt the same way but died before reaching the finish line.

One thing that Coach Marks had preached to Boots was not to look over his shoulder at the finish. "Keep running until you cross the finish line." So that was exactly what Boots did. When he crossed the finish line, he bent over and grabbed his knees. Coach Marks came running up and patted him on his back.

"Where did I finish?" Boots asked.

"Where did you finish?" Coach laughed. "You won by forty yards."

"You're kidding, aren't you?"

After the meet was over, Coach Marks drove Boots back to the plantation to replace Coach Richards on the work force.

As they drove up to the cotton field, there was Coach Richards bent over. He stood up, holding his back and wiping the sweat from his forehead.

"I sure hope he did well because this bending over has killed me. How can people do this every day?"

Coach Marks walked up, shaking his head. "Well, I wish you could have seen our boy."

"Well, quit beating around the bush. How did he do?"

"He won by forty yards," Marks said.

"What was his time?"

"That's what you're not going to believe," Coach Marks said. "He ran a 5:09.7"

"No way."

"I haven't told Boots yet, but this is the fastest time ever run in our conference," Coach Marks said.

He then turned to Boots and said, "Young man, the sky is the limit for you. If you can stay healthy, you can be one of the best runners in high school."

Boots went out into the field and started working. Coach Richards hobbled to his car and drove home. Coach Marks started home but saw Mr. Longhurst walking to his mailbox. He pulled over to talk to him.

He told Mr. Longhurst what had happened at the track meet. "This kid has more ability than any runner I have ever seen in any high school in the state of Mississippi, and I've coached for thirty years."

"So, what you were telling us last year is for real?" Mr. Longhurst asked.

"He is better than I even imagined. If he can keep healthy and keep his head right, he can be one of the best ever, at least in this state."

Boots ran in three more track meets before the county championship. Boots was never challenged. He won all, with room to spare.

Coach Marks decided to run Boots in more than one race in hopes of winning the conference championship. Boots won the mile and half mile in record times.

The following week, the district championships were held in a nearby town. To Boots's surprise, Mr. Longhurst had driven to see the meet. He also excused Coach Richards from working in Boots's place.

Coach Richards was most appreciative, since he had not been able to stand up straight since taking over for Boots.

Right before the race, Coach Marks walked over and told Boots that this was his chance to shine. He pointed to where Mr. Longhurst and the others were sitting in the stands. Tears began to build up in his eyes.

"No, none of this crying. You can cry after you win. Get your mind on the race."

The fastest time Boots had run in his three victories was 5:05. There were runners in the field who had run around 5:07, so he was going to have to work for it.

Through the first three laps, Boots was in fifth place. This was the hardest competition he had faced so far. He hadn't told anyone, but he wasn't feeling very well before the race. He thought it might be nerves, but he didn't think so. Since everyone had come to see him, he couldn't let them down.

Coming out of the second turn was where Boots usually began his kick; today, however, it just wasn't there. He began to feel like he couldn't finish. He couldn't let his friends and coaches down. He lowered his head and started running as hard as he could. He didn't open his eyes until he reached the third turn. Coming out of the last turn, he was even with at least one or two runners. He once again closed his eyes and ran as hard as he could. He ran ten yards past the finish line before he opened his eyes. He dropped to the ground and threw up. He had no clue where he had finished or if he could even get up. He knew he was sick, and it wasn't the race that made him sick.

Several coaches ran over to help him up. He could hardly stand on his own. He didn't know any of the coaches who were helping him, and all he wanted to do was lie down.

He finally recognized his coach's voice. "Please just let me lay down. I'm sick."

They helped Boots over to the outside of the track and let him lie there for several minutes. He still didn't know he had won by ten yards and had run the fastest mile in Mississippi history for a high school runner; 4:59.2 seconds. It was the third fastest in the United States that year by a high school runner, and he was still only a freshman.

Boots had the flu and was ordered to bed by Mr. Longhurst. He would have to run in the regionals the following Saturday. He also excused Coach Richards from working the next Saturday, which was the best news he had heard in a long time; he still couldn't stand up straight.

If somehow Boots could finish in the top three, he would qualify for the state meet the following week, which had never been achieved by a freshman in Mississippi history.

The fact that Boots was able to rest for most of the week without having to work on the farm helped him recover quicker than maybe he should have. The two coaches took turns bringing Boots a hot meal during their lunch periods to help him heal faster.

The regionals would be held about thirty miles away, so Coach Marks and Boots would have to leave very early to make sure they were there in time to stretch and warm up properly. To Coach Marks's surprise, he received a call from Mr. Longhurst saying that he would be attending the meet. Coach Marks thanked him for all his support and especially for allowing Coach Richards to not have to work in Boots's place.

Boots knew he was not at his best, and he also knew there were no bad runners in the field. Finishing in the top three and moving on to the state was everyone's goal for him. That was not his goal, however; he had come to win.

The race was different from all the others he had run. Normally, he would stay back and let other runners set the pace, and then he would come on at the end. Today, he found himself leading after the first lap; he wasn't sure what to do. He had always been back in the pack after the first lap. Were they letting him lead on purpose, trying to let him burn himself out, or was the pace just that slow? He normally waited until the last lap and the second turn to start his famous kick, but was he setting too fast of a pace and would he have his kick left? All these things were running through his mind. He had never experienced this kind of race before. Every time someone would pull even with him, he would think they were going to take the lead, but they would drop back. He was confused, never having been in this situation before.

As they approached the second turn, where he usually began his kick, three runners suddenly sprinted past him. He was caught off guard. He tried to stay calm and start his normal kick, but they seemed to be pulling away. He was in fourth place, which meant he would not qualify for the state meet.

He refocused his goal to pass just one of them. He closed his eyes on the backstretch and tried to remember his normal kick. As they entered the homestretch, there were four runners shoulder to shoulder. He was on the outside lane, but he noticed a couple of them fading, so he lunged for the finish line. He had never had to lean forward before, so he wasn't sure how to do it. He found himself tumbling over the finish line. He knew at least one of the runners was at his shoulder. He had no clue who had won.

Since there were no cameras in those days, the officials had to gather and decide who had won. It was ten minutes before a decision was made. The head official walked over to the announcer and handed him the results.

The stands grew quite as the announcer read the top five finishers, starting at number five, going down to number one. There was no question about the third, fourth, and fifth finishers. The question was, Who had won?

The second-place finisher was number twenty-one, and the winner was number twenty-six. Boots had to look down at his chest to remember what his number was; it was twenty-six. He had won. He was going to the state meet.

He dropped to his knees and felt his teammates' hugs and his coaches patting him on his back. He looked into Coach Marks's eyes, and they both felt the bond that had gotten them there. After the athletes stopped hugging him, Mr. Longhurst reached out and shook his hand and patted him on the back. He was on his way to climbing out of the miserable life his family had lived for generations.

After hearing his time of 5:06, Boots couldn't believe how slowly he had run. It felt like he had run his fastest mile, but it had been a struggle for some reason. He and Coach would try to figure out what had happened. He had won, which was the important thing, but he wasn't satisfied.

Boots was the first athlete in school history to qualify for the state meet. He was no longer the student no one paid attention to or made fun of; everyone wanted to be his friend.

The state meet would be held three hundred miles away, so most of his teammates and Mr. Longhurst would not be able to attend.

Coach Marks had never been to the state meet before, and Boots had never spent a night away from home, much less in a motel room. Boots had never eaten in a restaurant or seen a city with so many people walking around.

Boots and his coach had decided after the last race he should never lead at the beginning and set the pace for other runners but hang close and use his big kick at the end to blow the other runners away. This strategy had gotten him this far, so they felt it was his best hope for winning the school's first state championship.

The problem was another runner from upstate had the same strategy and was able to out-lean Boots at the finish line. Boots's dream of being undefeated and a state champion was over, at least for this year. He ran one of his slower times, which he couldn't understand. He felt like it was his best race, but it wasn't good enough.

This would be Boots's only loss in his high school career. He never lost another race in the next three years and won the state championship in the mile run. His senior year, he set a state record of 4:48.7. His problem now was which of the many offers he would accept to attend college. He would never pick cotton again.

At Boots's high school graduation, his mother and father—along with Mr. Longhurst—sat in the third row, clapping and cheering as Boots was handed his diploma. He entered high school as a nobody, but as he walked across the stage after receiving his diploma, he received the loudest applause of all the graduates.

Louise looked at Jim and said, "Well, the spell has been broken. We now have a high school graduate in the family."

Since this was a normal work day at the plantation, Jim said to Louise, "Let's go. I have to get back to work. I've already missed a half a day's work."

Mr. Longhurst said, "You have somewhere to go, but it is not work. I'm treating all three of you to lunch."

Boots knew that tomorrow he would be back to the same old grind that he had been brought up in. He was hoping to fill out some job applications around town, now that he was a graduate, to get an easier job. His life was about to change in another way.

Boots started receiving college offers from all over the country wanting him to come and run track for them.

Scholarships to colleges and universities were a lot different back in the fifties. Students received help with tuition, meals, books, and living quarters, but they had to work some form of a job to help pay a part of all the expenses.

Working a job and training was not a problem for Boots. He had been doing that for four years now. Any job he got would be a lot easier than the one he had now.

Since his parents knew nothing about colleges, he asked both his former coaches for advice and consulted Mr. Longhurst.

Boots was such a good runner he could go to any school he wanted, except the very high academic schools like Harvard, Yale, and Vanderbilt.

Boots really wanted to get out of Mississippi and see a new part of the country. He had never seen mountains or snow, but he didn't want to go to a place where the winters were really cold.

He narrowed his choices to Texas, Arkansas, Florida, and Tennessee.

Unlike recruiting today, everything was done by mail and telephone. Rarely did a track recruit get to go visit faraway schools.

He finally eliminated Texas and Florida because they had similar climates to where he was now. Arkansas was not much different in climate from the other two, so he tried to find out as much as he could about the University of Tennessee. He relied on Coach Marks for most of his information.

He found out that Tennessee had very good track and cross-country programs. They had won the SEC cross-country championship the year before and had one of the best 1,500-meter runners in the United States.

Boots wasn't sure if he would be required to run cross-country. He had never run over a mile in competition before, but he liked the idea of having one of the best 1500-meter runners in the country on the team. He would be an up-and-coming senior as Boots entered the program. It showed that the coach knew how to train 1500-meter runners, and Boots could probably gain a lot of valuable training techniques from the runner Butch Miller.

He asked Coach Marks if he could get as much information on the Tennessee track program as possible. He also wanted to know about the climate and weather in Tennessee.

He found out that the coach's name was John Sines. He was a highly respected coach, and he believed in God and in teaching his athletes how to become better athletes and people.

Boots was also told that the University of Tennessee was located in Knoxville, near the Smoky Mountains.

Boots thought, *Mountains and snow.*

Coach Marks called Coach Sines at Tennessee and set up a time that he and Boots could talk over the phone. Since Boots worked until after dark, it would have to be late at night or on a Sunday afternoon.

Coach Sines told Coach Marks that he required all his runners to attend Sunday-morning church services, and he always attended evening service, so it would have to be during the afternoon.

Since Boots had no phone, Coach Marks drove Boots over to his house so he could talk with Coach Sines.

As the talk was ending, Boots asked Coach Sines if he could talk it over with his parents before he gave him an answer.

Coach Sines said, "I want you to talk it over with your parents and tell them I will treat you like my own son. I'll praise and encourage you, but I will also discipline you if I need to."

When he got home that night, he told his parents about the conversation. He told them he wanted to go to the University of Tennessee.

They told him how proud they were of him, not just for his running accomplishment but also for being the first in the family to graduate from high school.

"You know that your father and I don't want you to leave, but even more, we don't want you to have to live the hard life we have lived."

Since they had no phone, they had to wait until Coach Marks came by to tell him the news.

Coach Marks was elated. He said, "Not only have I not had an athlete of Boots's ability, but to have him represent our small school and be known all over the United States is a coaching dream of mine. Can I set up another phone conversation between Boots and Coach Sines, so Boots can tell him the good news?"

The following night, Coach Sines heard the good news. He told Boots that even though he was recruiting him as a 1500-meter runner for the track team, he hoped he would run cross-country so it would build up his endurance for the 1500 meters.

"I'll mail you the papers you will need to sign to become a Volunteer."

Boots had never heard of a Volunteer. He had to ask Coach Marks what that meant.

Coach explained that it was the University of Tennessee's nickname. He told him about how soldiers from Tennessee had volunteered to serve under Gen. Andrew Jackson in the War of 1812 and performed under marked valor.

The papers were sent for Boots to sign. He was going to be a Volunteer.

As Louise was finishing up her duties at Mr. Longhurst's home, she heard someone yell to her. To her surprise, she saw Mr. Longhurst and his wife sitting in the yard under a tree, drinking lemonade. He motioned for her to come over.

"Has Boots decided anything about college yet?" he asked.

"Yes, sir. He has decided to go to the University of Tennessee. He got his papers to sign today. He doesn't even know he got them yet."

"Well then, we need to have a proper signing ceremony. You go out in the field and get Jim, and you two go home and freshen up and bring Boots for supper, and we will have a proper signing."

"You want us to eat supper in your house?" Louise asked.

"I sure do. You three have been loyal and hard workers for me, and I think we should celebrate. It is not every day a worker of mine signs a college scholarship. But don't tell Boots what it is about until we surprise him. Supper will be served at six."

"Thank you, Mr. Longhurst, but we don't have the proper clothes to wear for such an event."

"Nonsense. Wear whatever you like. Wear what you wore to Boots's graduation; those clothes looked nice. Who cares what you wear? It's a celebration, for Christ's sake. The boy did good. Let's show him we appreciate it."

Jim was hard at work in the fields. When he saw Louise approaching, he knew something was wrong. He saw Boots a few yards away, so he knew he was all right, but what could it be?

When Louise told Jim what Mr. Longhurst said, he couldn't believe it.

"Now you're not joshing me, are you, Mother?"

"No. I swear. I couldn't believe it either. We're not supposed to let Boots know what's going on. What reason can we use to tell him we're quitting early for?"

Jim thought a few seconds. "Just tell him Mr. Longhurst has some work for us to do in his house, and we need to look nice and proper to do whatever work he has for us."

26

Louise walked over and told Boots what his father had said to say.

"What do we need to get dressed up for? He has servants to do all that."

"I don't know, but we work for him. It beats being bent over out here in the field, working with this cotton."

Boots didn't know what was going on, but whatever it was would have to be better than working in the cotton field.

One the servants stopped by and told Louise that Mr. and Mrs. Longhurst would be expecting them for supper at six sharp.

It took only about five minutes to walk from their house to the Longhursts', so they left about ten minutes before six.

Boots still wasn't sure what was going on. He had never heard of workers being called out of the field to help with the Longhursts' dinner guest. He also couldn't figure out why his mother was carrying her pocketbook and a large envelope.

Upon entering the house, they were escorted to the dining room and shown where to sit.

Now Boots was really confused.

Mr. and Mrs. Longhurst walked in and greeted their guests.

"I thought we should perhaps explain to Mr. Boots here the purpose of our meeting before the meal is served, if that is all right with you Louise and Jim," Mr. Longhurst said. "Ms. Louise, will you do the honors?"

"James, we are all so proud of you, and the Longhursts were kind enough to ask that we tell you the good news over dinner," Louise said.

"What news?" Boots asked.

She handed him the large envelope she had been carrying and said, "This is why we are here celebrating tonight."

Boots opened the envelope and read that he had been accepted and was now on scholarship at the University of Tennessee's men's track team. All he had to do was sign, along with his parents, and mail the papers back to the university.

Everyone began cheering, even the servants. His mother bent over and kissed him on the head. His father shook his hand and turned away so no one would see the tears in his eyes.

Mr. Longhurst reached out and shook Boots's hand and told him how proud he was of all that he had accomplished.

"I expect to see you standing on the Olympic medal stand a few years from now," he said, laughing.

Boots began to cry and couldn't seem to stop. He couldn't believe that something so simple as running a race in the eighth grade had changed his life so drastically.

They all sat down and enjoyed the meal. The Harris family ate foods they had never eaten before, and they felt like really important people for the first time in their lives.

For at least one night in their lives, they weren't peasant workers on a plantation but normal people eating with their rich friends.

As they were leaving to go back to their home, Mr. Longhurst reached out and shook Boots's hand. He said, "When do I need to drive up and see you win the SEC 1500 meters championship? This year or next?"

"It might take a few years, but I'll give it my all," Boots replied.

Louise decided that Coach Richards and Coach Marks should be present as Boots signed his letter of intent. She also wanted Mr. Longhurst present. She wanted a picture, but she didn't know anyone who owned a camera. The signing was set for Sunday afternoon.

When she asked Mr. Longhurst if he would attend, she also reluctantly asked if he had a camera to take a picture of the signing.

He laughed and said he would not only bring his camera but also would make sure the picture was put in the local paper.

The following Sunday, everyone gathered for the signing and the pictures.

There was something everyone had forgotten about.

Coach Marks asked Boots when he was leaving and how he was getting there.

The Harrises had no car or any money for transportation to get Boots to Knoxville. They had overlooked the fact that Boots had to provide his own transportation to Knoxville, Tennessee.

No one knew how far it actually was or how much it would cost by bus or train.

The room remained silent for several seconds. The coaches were just barely getting by on their salaries, Boots's parents obliviously had no money, and they didn't expect their boss, Mr. Longhurst, to provide the money. No one had even thought about the expense of getting him there.

Finally, Jim said, "Mr. Longhurst, I know you don't ask your workers to work on Sunday, and I admire you for that, but is there anything I can do on Sundays to earn some extra money?"

Before he could answer, Coach Marks said, "I can't provide much, but I can chip in a little money."

"I can give some too," Coach Richards said.

"Wonder how much all this will cost?" Jim said.

"I'll call a friend of mine in the morning and find out," Mr. Longhurst said.

"I have an idea. Let Boots just run to Knoxville; that should get him in shape for the upcoming season." Coach Richards laughed.

The following day, Mr. Richards walked out in the field where Jim was working and said, "Don't worry. Boots's ticket to Knoxville has been bought. He leaves next Saturday. Go Vols."

"Did you pay for it? I'll work it off," Jim replied.

"I said it had been paid for. You don't worry about who paid for it," Mr. Longhurst said. "Like I told him, I plan on being there when he steps upon the podium as the SEC 1500-meter champion."

The following Saturday, Boots was ready to start a new life. He was scared and nervous. The greatest distance he had ever been away from home was at the state track meet a few hundred miles away. Now he was traveling several states away to a state he had never even seen before.

He would be experiencing a completely different lifestyle from the one he had grown up in, and he would be taking college courses he didn't know if he could handle. Needless to say, he was scared.

Since freshman were not eligible to compete, he would have a year of training to get used to major changes that were about to take place in school and prepare to compete at the college level.

As he stepped off the bus, he was greeted by a man wearing a Tennessee sweatshirt. The man introduced himself as Mike Turner, the assistant track coach at the University of Tennessee.

"James or Boots? Which do you go by?" Turner asked.

"I've been called Boots so long I almost don't remember my real name, sir. It's a pleasure to meet you, Mr. Turner," Boots replied.

"Just call me Coach; only ones who ever call me Mr. Turner are a few of my flock."

Boots wasn't sure what he was talking about. "I'm not sure I understand. Why would you have a flock?"

"Oh, I'm sorry. In addition to being on the coaching staff at UT, I am also a pastor," Turner replied.

Boots had never heard of a pastor-coach before.

"So, if you are ready, we will drive you to your new home," Coach said. "How did you get the nickname Boots?"

He explained how his boots were once the only shoes he had and about having to run in some kind of fitness test, so everyone started calling him Boots.

As they were driving along, Boots was fascinated by all the hills and mountains.

"Mr. Turner."

"Just call me Coach. Everyone does," Turner replied.

"Sorry. Coach, why are all of these mountains on fire?"

"On fire?" Then Coach realized why he would think they were on fire. "All the things that look like smoke are really just clouds and fog rising from the mountains. There is such a temperature change from the mountains to the flat lands that it just looks like smoke. That's why this region is called the Smoky Mountains."

"When will it snow?" Boots asked.

"It will be several months yet before that happens. Do you like snow?"

"I've never seen snow, Coach," Boots replied.

Coach had forgotten that not everyone lived where there was snow. "So, you've never made a snowman or had a snowball fight?"

"No, sir," Boots replied. "What is a snowball fight, sir?"

Coach explained a snowball fight, and riding a sled, and skiing down those big mountains. "I'll take you to one of the ski slopes around here when it snows, and you can watch. But you cannot ski. Too much chance of injury.

"Your roommate is named Paul Gentry. He will be a sophomore this year and will be able to compete in cross-country and track."

They pulled into a large parking garage, and coach pointed out a large building and said that would be his home for the next four years.

Boots was already homesick and wasn't sure he should have left Mississippi after all.

It didn't take him long to unload his belongings. He had only a small bag of clothes. He had left those boots behind, which now were starting to fit his feet after all the years of wearing them.

Coach led Boots to room twenty-six and knocked on the door. Coach introduced him to his new roommate for at least the next three years.

"You can get settled in, and Paul can show you were the cafeteria is later. Welcome to the University of Tennessee, son. We are glad to have you here," Coach said as he was leaving.

Boots and Paul carried on small talk as Boots was putting away his few clothes.

"One thing you're going to find out about living here is everyone is so friendly. People will smile and wave at you and say *howdy* and *you-all* a lot. The South is a lot different from where I come from up north," Paul explained.

"If you're hungry, we can go to the cafeteria and eat anytime."

Boots was always hungry. The three meals a day he had gotten at home since he graduated were not enough to fill him up; he missed the meals at school that the coach had secretly paid for.

"Here is the lunch card that Coach Sines left for you. You just show it to the lady at the cash register, and she stamps it, and you go on and eat."

"I thought you ran cross-country as well as track," Boots said.

"I do."

"But I thought Coach Sines was supposed to be at a cross-country meet today. Why aren't you there too?" Boots asked.

"Oh, it wasn't a big meet, and Coach said he would rather I stay here today and help you get settled in."

As they were going through the lunch line, Boots wasn't sure how much food he was allowed to get, so he just got basically the same thing Paul did.

When they sat down at the table, Boots noticed that some of the bigger guys had their plates crammed full of food. He asked Paul who those guys were, and he was told they were football players and they ate a lot.

Boots had never had that much food in two days, much less in one meal.

When they got back to the room, there stood Coach Sines outside the door.

Boots had never met the coach before, even though they had talked on the phone a couple of times.

They went into the room, and Paul went over to his desk and began to study for his classes.

Coach sat down with Boots and went over the things he needed to do to start classes. He was to go see a guidance counselor by the name of

Mr. Winkle. He would help him decide the courses to take and explain how to get his college life headed in the right direction.

Coach also told Boots that he wanted him to run with the cross-country team to build up his endurance and stamina. He was told that freshman weren't allowed to participate in varsity sports, but it would really help him when track season came around next year.

He also said that he required all of his runners to attend church on Sundays. He explained that the ones who did not attend a home church could ride a van to hear Coach Turner's services.

"Running is important, but your soul is more important. You can't run all of your life, but you can serve God all of your life," Coach said.

The following morning after eating in the cafeteria, Paul showed Boots where he needed to go to met with his guidance counselor.

Boots walked out and sat down on a bench to view his schedule. He had English, math, history, health, PE, and a science class. He knew he would have to put a lot more effort into his schoolwork than he had in the past, and even though he would be training a lot, he knew it had to be easier than working in that cotton field from daylight until dark.

He decided to walk around campus and try to find out where his classes would be held.

He could see the giant football stadium in the distance, so he decided to go look at it. Until then, he had never noticed that there was a large river running right beside the university. He saw both big and small boats heading up and down it.

He also noticed that everyone seemed really friendly and usually spoke to him if he was looking at them. This was not what he was used to.

When he was next to the football stadium, he couldn't believe how large it was. He couldn't go inside, but he could see that it probably held thousands of people.

Since this was sort of a free day before classes started, he decided to see if he could find the track he would be running on in the future. He asked someone who looked like an athlete if he knew where the running track was, and the student pointed the direction it was in.

When he reached the track, there were runners already running on it. He had never seen a track so beautiful. It was even better than the track he ran the state meet on back home.

He saw Coach Turner standing on the side of the track with a stopwatch in his hand. He was timing some runners who were running sprints.

He decided to move a little closer, hoping that Coach Turner might see him.

The runners crossed the finish line, and the coach showed them the stopwatch and told them it was a good workout and to go take a shower.

Boots stepped onto the track and bent down and felt how smooth it was.

"You're next, Boots. Got the watch on you."

He looked over to see Coach Turner smiling at him.

Coach walked over, put his arm around him, and asked how his first day went.

"This is a big place. I have never seen anything like the football stadium and these big buildings. I saw the river for the first time today. It is unbelievable."

"So, are you ready to start classes tomorrow?"

"I guess so. It's sort of intimidating by how big this place is and how many students go here," Boots replied.

"You'll fit right in. May take you a few days to get used to it. Have you been told what your job will be yet?"

"No, Coach, I haven't. I'm sort of worried about that too."

"The job won't be a problem. The work is not hard. You'll be fine."

"Coach and I will meet with the new runners on Wednesday to explain the training and such. We'll let you know sometime tomorrow. Your dorm will have a mailbox with your name on it, so you can get mail from home, and we can leave messages in your box if need be."

As he turned and started walking back to his dorm, he hoped he had made the right decision in coming here. The hills and mountains were so beautiful, and everyone seemed so friendly. Things were just so much more fast-paced. He was used to going to school and then working in the fields until dark. The only people he ever saw after school were the other workers, and they were always sad and tired.

He decided to see if he could remember where the cafeteria was and eat before he went back to the dorm. That was another good thing about being here; the food was good, and he could eat three meals a day every day.

His schedule had him going to three classes on Monday, Wednesday, and Friday. He had two classes on Tuesday and Thursday. He would be required to work at whatever job they gave him for three hours a day. Then he would have his track workouts. It sounded like a long day until he remembered being in the fields working cotton and tobacco. *This schedule isn't so bad after all*, he thought.

After his classes were over for the day, he went to lunch and back to the dorm. He found his mailbox, and in it were two notes. One was from Coach Shines, telling him to be at the track at three, and they would begin going over the workout schedule for the week. The other note was from the library, saying his job would be working for them. He needed to bring this slip of paper to the front desk at the library on Wednesday after his last class, and they would tell him what he would be doing. He had not been expecting a job in the library. He thought it would be more like working in the cafeteria, cleaning up dirty tables.

He got his food and went over to find a table with no one at it, but there weren't any. He sat at a table with three other students.

It wasn't long before they struck up a conversation with him. He was not used to people being this friendly, especially to a stranger.

When he got back to his room, Paul was not there, so he decided to lie down on the bed and read one of his assigned readings from his science class that morning.

As he opened the book, he couldn't remember the last time he was able to lie in a bed before it was dark outside. It was also weird not going out and running. He had to leave his track shoes at the high school when he graduated.

Paul walked in and asked him how his day had gone.

He told him about the job at the library.

Paul laughed. "You got one of those pie jobs."

Boots had never heard the term *pie jobs*, so he didn't know if that meant it was good or bad.

The following morning, he attended his classes and then had to ask someone where the library was.

He took the note to the front desk and showed it to the lady at the counter.

"Just a minute, and I'll get Ms. Watson."

He saw an elderly woman walking up to the front desk with the note he had given to the other woman.

"Hi. I'm Ms. Watson. Let's go over here and sit down at the table, and I'll explain your job to you."

She explained that he would load up the books that had been returned by students and put them back on the shelves in their proper place.

She went over and got a few books out of the return bin and showed Boots the numbers on the books. She then showed him how each row of books was numbered and how to put the books on shelves according to the numbers on the other books.

"That's all I have to do? Just put books back on the shelves?" Boots asked.

"Yes, you see, it is not a hard job. When you get here after class, there might be a few books but never more than ten or fifteen. Someone else has the same job in the morning, so they have the most books to handle. You'll have a lot of free time to sit and do your classwork or just read."

"After your last class, just go eat lunch and come over when you get through. Your job says to work three hours a day, but we don't punch a time clock. I know you are an athlete and have training to do, so if you need to leave after a couple of hours, that's fine. Just tell me or someone you need to leave, and it will be okay."

Boots met with his coaches and received his shoes and practice uniforms, along with sweat suits to run in outdoors when it was cold.

Boots trained with the cross-country team and was allowed to run in some meets, even though he did not count in the team's scoring. Boots was already the third best runner on the team; the other two runners were both seniors.

Since he didn't have any money and his parents didn't have a car or money, they had to communicate mostly by letters.

When he experienced his first measurable snow, he was like a kid at Christmas. He went out and rolled in it and helped some of the other students make a snowman. The day ended in a snowball fight. Boots couldn't wait to write it all down and mail it to his parents.

Coach Turner had all the track athletes that could not go home for Christmas over at his house for Christmas dinner.

Since all the track athletes were required to attend a church service, Boots had learned more about God and the Bible than he had ever heard at home. Since Sunday afternoon was their only day off, his parents rarely attended formal church services, but they were both believers in God.

Boots believed in God; he just hadn't made a commitment to him yet.

Boots learned a lot about running from the coaches and the older runners. He just wished he could run in meets like the upperclassmen. He couldn't wait for next year to start.

As his first school year was ending, he had learned how to become a better student, and he didn't miss the cotton fields one bit.

He could stay and attend summer school and work part-time away from the school, or he could just get a job and work, but his room and board would not be paid for. He decided to take just enough classes to qualify to keep his room and board. Coach Sines got him a job on the weekends so he could earn enough money for a bus ticket home for next Christmas to see his family.

As the new school year started, Boots couldn't wait. He had come to school to run, but it wasn't a lot of fun being a freshman and not being able to compete. He thought it was a stupid rule. If you were able to go to school, why shouldn't you be eligible to compete just like the upperclassmen?

Boots finished his cross-country season winning three of the four meets he ran in. He finished fifth in the SEC championship.

Boots was able to go home and see his parents and former coaches at Christmas. Mr. Longhurst told him he had been following his career and had even bought a Tennessee sweatshirt and had been wearing it around town.

When it came time to say goodbye, Boots didn't want to leave. He loved the college life, but he missed seeing his parents. He could see that with the hard life they had been living, they were aging a lot faster than they should.

When he returned to start the spring semester, the winter was cold, and a lot of workouts took place indoors.

Boots was told he would be running the 800 and 1500 meters at the track meets.

He would have to run a lot of sprints and 400-meter sprints to build up his speed. Other days, he would have to run long distances to build up his endurance.

Before he knew it, the first track meet was here. It would be a three-way meet between Virginia, Vanderbilt, and Tennessee.

Boots was so nervous he had trouble breathing. It had been two years since he had run a real track meet that counted.

The coaches had been working on him going out at a faster pace and still having enough left for his famous three-quarter last lap kick.

As the gun sounded, Boots was almost knocked to the ground as runners fought for position going into the first turn.

Boots stayed near the front until the backstretch of the last lap when he started pulling away. He won by ten yards.

The 800 was added to Boots's events to help score points for his team; his real specialty was the 1500 meters, which was basically the same as the mile run. Since most of the world used meters, most of the teams in the US had started running their meets in meters as well.

Boots would have about an hour to rest and then start loosening up for the 1500.

Tennessee's two best runners in the 1500 meters had graduated, and there was not anyone but Boots who could possibly score the points that UT would need in the meets that were to come, especially the SEC championships.

As the gun sounded, Boots was in the lead going into the first turn. He was still leading after laps two and three. He remembered another time this had happened back in high school; he hoped he still had a kick left.

When he reached the backstretch of the last lap, he started his famous kick. He didn't look over his shoulder to see where the other runners were; he just put his shoulders back and ran as hard as he could.

When he crossed the finish line, he had won by twenty-five yards.

His time was 4:35.7. This was the fastest he had ever run, and this was his second race of the meet.

The same thing occurred in the next three meets they had. He lowered his time to 4:34.5. He now had the fastest time in the SEC.

He had the fifth best time in the United States.

Boots entered the SEC championships having finished second one time in the 800 meters and undefeated in the 1500 meters.

The year before, Ed Murphey had won the 1500-meter SEC championship for Tennessee. Murphey had now graduated, but he had helped Boots develop into the runner he was today, so he hoped he could carry on the tradition.

"Runners, take your mark," the starter said.

"Set."

Bang—the pistol barked.

Boots had to keep himself calm. He wanted to get the lead and blow the field away, but he knew there were several runners who would go out too fast, then fade away. He had to run a smart race, and taking the lead at this point wasn't smart.

By the end of the first lap, the lead runner had already died and pulled off the track. His purpose was to run a fast pace and try to get the other runners to fall for his ploy; then they would burn themselves out, and his teammate could move up and hopefully score points for their team.

Boots started the second lap in seventh place, which was farther back than he hoped to be.

By the end of the second lap, two more runners had slowed, and he now was in fifth.

This was where he hoped his 800-meter training would help. He moved out to the second lane and started running faster than he normally would. He had to be careful and not run so fast he would not have his normal kick down the backstretch.

As they crossed the finish line after the third lap, Boots was in third place. He pulled up even with the runner in second as they came out of the second turn. This was where he usually started his final kick. He felt like he might have gone out too fast earlier in the race. He kept telling himself he could be in a cotton field picking cotton right now, and he thought of his parents working from daylight until dark. He closed his eyes and ran as hard as he could. He would either finish or pass out trying.

Entering the third turn, he was a body length behind the first-place runner.

As they turned down the homestretch, he closed his eyes and ran as hard as he could. He opened his eyes about ten yards from the finish, and he could see the other runner through his peripheral vision.

He saw the finish line approaching, so he leaned so far that he fell face-first across the finish line. He was now an SEC champion.

His time was 4:35.9.

He was helped up by some of the other runners, and as he walked toward the stands, he was mobbed by his coaches and teammates.

Even though he was so tired he could hardly stand up, he thought, *This beats picking cotton.*

When the initial congratulations had calmed down from everyone, Boots started walking by himself to cool down and loosen his legs up, since they were starting to feel tight and began to ache a little.

He was looking forward to some much-needed rest after a long season. He had trained for more than two years for this race, and now he could relax and take some time off.

As he was nearing the team area, he saw Coach Turner walking toward him.

"You know what you've done, don't you?" he asked.

"Sure, Coach, I won. I'm the SEC champion," Boots replied.

"I'm not talking about that," Coach said.

Boots didn't know what he was talking about. He was afraid he had done something wrong.

"No. What, Coach? Am I in trouble for something?"

"So, you really don't know?"

"No, Coach. What is going on?" Boots asked.

"Your winning time qualifies for the NCAA championships. We're going to Austin, Texas."

Boots didn't say anything; he was thinking, *That is near home. Maybe I can see my parents.*

"So, aren't you happy?" Coach asked.

"Sure, but I hadn't even thought about the NCAAs. I thought my season would be over after today. Texas is near Mississippi, and I know they can't afford it, but it would be nice for my parents to be able to see me run. They are getting pretty feeble from working on that plantation all of their lives. My father can't even stand up straight anymore."

As he was standing on the awards stand and they were awarding him his medal, he thought about the day he first ran a race in the eighth grade, wearing those big boots; he had come a long way, and he was proud but humble.

That night, after the team had eaten and returned to their rooms, a bellhop knocked on Boots's door and said he needed to come to the lobby. He had a phone call from home.

Boots was scared. He was afraid something had happened to his mother or father. He knew they didn't have a phone, so it couldn't be good.

When he picked up the phone, he heard his mother and father yelling, "We are the parents of an SEC champion!"

Mr. Longhurst had arranged the phone call and told Boots how proud they all were of him. He said, "We might live in Mississippi, but we were sure pulling for Tennessee in this race. I'd say the sale of Tennessee sweatshirts will go up around here." He laughed.

His parents and Mr. Longhurst were all trying to listen on the phone. They had it held in the middle with everyone's head turned toward the receiver, trying to hear the conversation.

"Well, I've got some more good news. My winning time was good enough to qualify me for the NCAA championships in Austin, Texas."

Boots heard laughter and cheering through the phone.

"Why, that's only a couple hundred miles from here," Mr. Longhurst said. "Maybe I can get down to see you."

Boots had hoped he would say, "Maybe we could get down to see you," but he knew his parents couldn't afford a trip like that.

After he hung up, he went back and lay down on his bed and began to think about all that had happened in the last twenty-four hours. He had to wipe a tear from his eye.

The following Sunday at church, Coach Sines and Pastor Turner recognized the track team and Boots for winning the 1500-meter.

After the service, Boots thanked Coach Turner for what he had said and the training he had helped him with.

Pastor Turner said, "Well, as proud of you as we are, you do realize that your eternal destiny is a lot more important than a race around a track. I want you to think about that. As you become more famous, people are going to want to be around you, and some of those people are like leeches. They will pull you down to their level, and that is not good. Just be careful of who you run around with." He reached over and hugged Boots.

Boots didn't say anything, but he had sort of already experienced some of the wild crowd. He had been invited to a party on Saturday night, and he had never drunk beer before, but it was free, and everyone was drinking, so he joined in. He had even considered skipping church this morning because of the hangover he had. He lost count of how many times he had thrown up during the night.

The following Monday, Coach Sines met with the five athletes who had qualified for the NCAAs. He went over their training schedules with each individual. To Boots's surprise, his training was much less than normal. He thought he should be training harder for the bigger meet.

The following day at the track, he was told that Coach Turner would oversee his training for the next few days. The meet in Texas would be in three weeks.

"Coach, I don't understand why I am training less for this meet. Shouldn't I be training more?" Boots asked.

The coach explained that he had been training so hard for the SEC meet that his body needed to rest and repair itself. Running fewer miles and training less would give his body time to recover before the big race.

The NCAAs would take place after the spring semester of classes were over. Boots had decided to not take classes but work during the summer to try to save some money.

Boots received a letter in the mail from Mr. Longhurst, who offered him a summer job being a foreman on his plantation. He wouldn't have to do any physical labor, just train and see that everything that needed to be done on the farm was done.

Boots went and talked to Coach Shines and showed him the letter.

"Sounds like a pretty good deal. Just make sure you do your workouts each day."

"Well, here is what I was wondering, Coach. My home is only a few hundred miles from Austin. It doesn't make much sense to travel all the way back here after the meet and turn around and have to pay to go all the way back down there to spend the summer. Is there any way I could take the bus from Austin to my home? It would save me a lot of money. Plus, it would save the school money too, because they wouldn't have to feed me on the way back."

The coach sat there and thought a few minutes. "I don't see why we couldn't do that. School is officially out anyway, so you're technically on your own after the meet. Sounds like a good idea. I know it will make your parents happy."

Boots couldn't wait to get back to his dorm and write Mr. Longhurst and thank him for the job. He also wrote his parents and told them the good news.

Boots started to see what Coach Turner had talked about. Everyone seemed to know who he was now. People wanted to stop and talk to him and have pictures taken with him. He was invited to all kinds of parties. He still had not recovered from the last party. He vowed to himself he would never drink that much again.

His training had begun as soon as they got back from the SEC meet. Since most of the track athletes had not qualified for the NCAA meet, the coaches could work more individually with the ones who had. Boots was the only runner Coach Turner was to work with.

Even though the workouts were not as strenuous, Boots's legs still felt heavy and tired. He hoped this would go away before the meet, because he had never felt this fatigued before.

At practice the following day, he was told to report to the swimming pool instead of the track. Tennessee had a great swim team, but he had no idea why he was there.

Coach Turner told him he would be running in the pool today.

Boots thought he was joking, but he was serious.

The coach explained that running across the pool in the shallow end would provide a workout but also help his legs get a rest from the normal workouts.

Boots thought they were crazy, but the following day, his legs and body did feel a lot better. He felt like he did after taking a day off from workouts.

As time drew nearer for the meet, he was told to just lie on his bed and rest his legs. He didn't have to sleep but just stay off his feet as much as possible.

Since school was out and he didn't have to work at the library every day, he didn't know what to do with himself. He began reading a lot of books. One of the books he read was *The Power of Positive Thinking* by Norman Vincent Peale. It had been given to him by Coach Turner.

Coach Turner had become one of Boots's favorite people. He was demanding as far as making him work on the track, but he was caring and kind. He kept telling Boots that the life after our earthly one is the most important. Boots figured he was right, but he had a lot of other things he needed to worry about more, and he could worry about that when he got old and was ready to die.

As they were getting ready to leave for the NCAAs, Boots was feeling better than he had in months. His legs no longer felt tired and heavy.

He was also looking forward to traveling to see his parents after the meet and starting his new job on the plantation.

Because of all the equipment they had to take, the team would be transported to Austin in school vans. They would leave several days early so their bodies would have time to get over the long trip. There were only four athletes going, as one was injured in training.

After the long journey to Austin, they were finally ready to see the track where the competition would take place.

Boots would not run until the third day after the meet started. Many of the races would require several heat races. A runner would have to finish in the top three to advance to the next heat.

Boots would not have to run any heat races. Since the qualifying times for the 1500 were so low, there were only twelve men in the country who met the qualifying times, so there was no need for heats in the 1500.

Boots wanted to contact his parents, but even though they were so close as far as distance went, they had no phone, so it was still like they were a world away.

He knew that they would not be able to see him run. Even if the race was on TV, they had no television. He thought that maybe Mr. Longhurst might invite them over to see the sports news, and they might show or say something about the race, but Mr. Longhurst had said he would be in Austin to see the race, so he felt sad that his parents would know nothing until someone told them.

Boots sat in the stands with the coaches and the other athletes from Tennessee who had made the trip and watched the first two days of events.

The day of Boots's event, the team arrived several hours early. Boots was really nervous and tense. He had never been involved in an event this big.

Coach Sines told Boots that he needed to talk to him behind the stadium. Boots assumed they would be talking over strategy for the race.

As they walked around the corner, there stood Mr. Longhurst. Boots walked up to shake his hand, but Mr. Longhurst put his arms around Boots and hugged him.

Boots thanked him for coming and then asked how his parents were doing.

"I don't know. Why don't you ask them yourself?"

Boots turned around to see his parents standing behind him.

They ran up and hugged him, and they all had tears in their eyes.

Boots turned to Mr. Longhurst and said, "Thank you so much for bringing them. I don't know what to say."

"Well, you need to hear the real story of what happened. Coach Sines, do you want to tell the story?"

"Coach Turner heard that your parents could probably not attend (he didn't want to embarrass his parents by saying couldn't afford), so he told his Wednesday-night congregation, and they spread the word throughout the church, and they took up a collection to send to your parents so they could ride the bus down here to see you run. When Mr. Longhurst heard about it, he offered to drive your parents, and they could save the bus fare. Everyone wins."

Tears began to form in Boots's eyes. His father said, "None of that stuff. You have a race to run."

Boots needed to go start loosening up, but he had to find Coach Turner first and thank him.

The coach didn't want any credit; he said it was the people at the church who did it all. Boots knew better though.

Boots knew he would have to run the race of his life. His fastest time in the 1500 meters of 4:34 was at one time one of the fastest in the United States, but since all the conference championships had been run in the last month, it was only fourth best in the field of twelve.

Boots had not come here to finish toward the back of the field, especially knowing his parents were in the stands watching him.

As he stepped to the line, he asked God to help him do well for his parents, coaches, and all the people back at the church who had been so kind. He usually only prayed if he was in trouble. He wasn't sure how this prayer stuff worked. He thought he had heard that God only answered prayers of his children. He was brought back to the present when he heard the starter say, "Set," and then the gun went off.

Going into the first turn, there was a lot of pushing and shoving. Coach Sines had warned him about that and to stay back and watch for any runners that might fall.

Coming out of the second turn, he was in last place. He knew he had been running too slow, so he tried to move up a couple of positions, but he was still in last place after the first lap.

As the second and third laps were completed, he had been able to move up into sixth place. He normally started his kick coming out of the second turn of the final lap, but he felt like he needed to start it now. He had never started his kick so early, so he didn't know if he could make it that far. He remembered that when he had run the half mile, the pace had to be quicker, so he decided to chance it.

Heading into the third turn, he was in fifth place and closing on the runner in front of him. As they crossed the finish line, he leaned across the line. He knew he had not won, but he had no idea where he had finished.

As he bent over with his hands on his knees, an official walked up and put his hands on his back and told him he had finished third with a time of 4:31.1. He had beaten his time by three seconds.

He looked up in the stands to see his mother, father, and Mr.

Longhurst jumping up and down, cheering. He noticed that in addition to Mr. Longhurst wearing a Tennessee shirt, his mother and father had one on too.

When he got to his coaches, they were both elated.

Coach Sines said, "The two guys who beat you are both seniors, and the fourth, fifth, and sixth runners are seniors too. So, you know what we are expecting next year, don't you?"

Boots spent the summer working for Mr. Longhurst. The job was just like he had described it to him. He just had to see that things ran smoothly, and he didn't have to do any of the hard work he used to have to do.

He found out that his father was in a lot worse shape than he had imagined. In those days, people working on plantations did not have a certain age they could retire at and get government assistance like they do today.

While working throughout the summer, Boots continued his workouts. He had forgotten how hot it could get in the summer in Mississippi.

He had saved most of his money, but he had tried to help his parents by buying them some things they had never been able to afford.

The night before he had to leave, his mother cooked a big meal and invited Coach Richards and Coach Marks, along with Mr. Longhurst and his wife.

Boots was surprised to see that Mr. Longhurst and his wife had come. He thought they would be ashamed to be seen in one of their tenants' houses, but they seemed right at home.

Goodbyes were said, and Boots climbed aboard the bus heading back to Tennessee. He hated to leave, but he also missed his new home in Tennessee.

On the long bus ride, Boots reminisced about when he started running in the eighth grade and how he was considered a nobody and made fun of and now how everyone wanted to talk to him and be around him. He also remembered what Coach Turner had said about the leeches that would pull him down. He knew that would never happen to him.

It was good seeing his coaches and fellow runners again.

They would officially start training for cross-country the following week, when school started. He would also start his old job in the library.

Some of his teammates invited him to a party to usher in the coming school year. Boots reluctantly agreed to go, but he vowed to himself he would not drink like he had the year before. He could still remember how sick he was following the party the last time.

The following morning after the party, Boots woke up with a headache, like he had before. He didn't throw up this time, and he hadn't drunk as many beers, so he thought that was a plus. He was still amazed by how many people wanted to be around him and talk to him. He still didn't think any of them were the leeches Coach Turner had talked about.

Boots breezed through the cross-country season, winning every meet. A few days before the SEC cross-country championships, Boots and his teammates were out training in the mountains when Boots turned his ankle as he stepped on a rock. It became apparent he could not run in the SEC championship. He had been favored to win, but he watched from the sidelines while on crutches. He would miss a month of training after that. His running started out in the swimming pool, like he had done the year before.

Just before Christmas break, another setback occurred.

Boots's father passed away. He had to take the long bus ride back to Mississippi to attend the funeral.

While he was there, he saw how fragile his mother's health was, and he decided he would not return to school but stay and take care of his mother. He knew he would have to go back to work on the plantation until he could find a better job.

He talked to Mr. Longhurst about a job. Mr. Longhurst asked Boots if he had discussed this with his mother. He told him he would always have a job for him, but he needed to talk it over with his mother first.

When Boots told his mother about his plans, she immediately shut down those thoughts in a hurry. She told him he was not quitting school, and he was not going to stay and take care of her; she was able to take care of herself. She went on to say that she had been taking care of not only herself but also his father.

"If I need help, I'll let you know, but you're not quitting school. You have made your father and me so proud that you have made something of yourself. Mr. Longhurst has already told me I don't need to work if I don't feel like it, and he will help me if I need it."

Boots reluctantly boarded the bus and headed back to school. He dreaded going back and leaving his mother; he also hated to see winter coming up. He liked seeing the snow and all the activities that went with it, but he was down because of the death of his father and the health of his mother.

When he walked into his dorm room, his roommate told him that Coach Turner needed to see him as soon as he got back. He said he would be in the coach's office.

When he walked into the office, he told Boots to shut the door behind him. Boots knew something was wrong.

"Boots, sit down. I need to talk to you. I'm talking to you now as your pastor more than your friend and coach. While you were on the bus trip home, your mother passed away."

Boots was speechless. How could this be happening? Boots lowered his head and started sobbing.

Pastor Turner walked over and put his hands on Boots's shoulder and told him how sorry he was.

Coach Sines, who had been waiting in his office, waited until Coach Turner had told Boots the bad news and then walked in and offered him his sympathy as well.

After talking to Boots for several minutes, he was told he could fly back for his mother's funeral. Boots told them he couldn't afford to fly. They showed him the airplane ticket that had already been purchased for him. He asked where the money came from, and they just said, "Friends."

Boots was driven to the airport the following day by Coach Turner. Boots had never been to an airport, much less flown on a plane before.

Boots had taken the money he had earned while working for Mr. Longmire out of the bank and had it with him. He didn't know what kind of expenses he would face. He knew he would have to hire a cab just to get out to the plantation, which was nowhere near the airport. He had no clue how much a taxi cost.

The plantation had a cemetery that dated back to the 1800s. Workers had been buried in it for generations. Most were put in wooden boxes with just a wooden cross over the grave. His father had been buried there a little over a week ago, and now his mother.

He had saved his money, hoping to maybe buy a cheap car. Here he was a junior in college, and he had never driven a car or had a driver's license.

Mr. Longhurst had already had some of his men dig the grave. There were caskets in an old store room that were built by one of the workers. People had been dying on the plantation for years, so they always needed to keep a supply ready. No one who worked on the plantation could afford a real funeral.

Mr. Longhurst told Boots to box up the things he wanted to keep of his parents, and he would store them in one of the buildings until he finished college.

After the funeral, Boots went started packing things in some old wooden crates he found in the barn. There were a lot of things that were just junk, so he left it for whoever would move into the house next. He thought, *Some people's junk is someone else's treasure.*

Mr. Longhurst dropped by to see how Boots was doing. Boots told him he would be flying back the next day. When he was asked how he was getting to the airport, he told Mr. Longhurst he would have to call a cab and asked if might use a phone the following morning.

"Nonsense. I'll have Barney drive you to the airport. What time is your flight?"

"It's at 11:20," Boots replied.

"I'll have Barney here by ten; that will give you plenty of time."

"Thank you for all you have done for me and my parents. I really appreciate it."

"Your parents were two of my best workers. I liked them both. You keep in touch with me and let me know how things are going. You have my address and phone number, so I'll look forward to hearing from you. I'll be wearing my Tennessee shirt when you have a big meet," Mr. Longhurst said.

Boots wasn't taking much that belonged to his parents back to school with him, but he did have the two Tennessee shirts packed that they had worn when he ran in Austin. That was the only time they had ever seen him run. *And the last*, he thought.

After he landed at the airport, he was heading to find a taxi when he saw Coach Turner walking up to him.

"What are you doing here?" Boots asked.

"I knew when your plane was scheduled to land, so I thought you might need a ride," he said.

Coach didn't want to bring anything up about his mother's death, so he just asked him how he liked flying in a plane.

"The next time, I'll just take the bus or walk," Boots said. "I looked out of the window a few times, and my heart almost stopped beating."

The students were to get out for Christmas holidays in a couple of days, so Boots didn't know what he was supposed to do about the classes he had missed. If he didn't get the credits, he would not be eligible for the coming track season.

When they arrived at the coach's office, he asked the coach what he should do about the classes he had missed.

"Don't worry. We have already talked to all of your teachers, and they are going to work with you to catch you up on what you've missed. You just need to go and talk to them, and they will work with you."

When he got back to his dorm room, he saw his roommate's suitcase open on his bed. He knew he was packing to leave for Christmas break.

Boots lay down on his bed and looked at the ceiling. This would be his first Christmas with his parents now gone. All the students were preparing to go home for Christmas, and he would be left alone in the dorm over the holidays. He finally drifted off to sleep.

The following day, he began to contact all of his teachers. Since there were still a few days of classes left, he had to wait until the teachers weren't in class teaching; so it turned into an all-day affair.

The professors were very kind and willing to work with him since they all knew the circumstances behind his absences. Some even told him he wouldn't have to take the final test; they would just give him a grade on the work he had done prior to leaving.

As the week of Christmas approached, he had made up all of his work. He had not been running in almost three weeks, so he decided to get back in shape and forget about Christmas. That was easier said than done, as everywhere he went or ran, there were all kinds of Christmas directions.

Coach Turner invited Boots over to his house on Christmas Eve, and Coach Sines had him over on Christmas Day. Each family had a gift for Boots, which made him sad because he hadn't gotten anything for them.

January finally arrived, and a new semester of classes and track workouts were set to begin. He had been running on his own for a few weeks, but he felt so out of shape he was dreading the first day of workouts.

He would be the defending SEC 1500-meter champion, and anything less than repeating as a junior would be considered a failure. Even though he told no one, his personal goal was to break the four-minute mile. He needed to lower his best time by more than thirty-one seconds, which didn't sound like much, but it was going to be a big challenge.

After three months of hard training, the first meet arrived. Once again, he ran the 800 and 1500 meters. He knew running the 800 would help him be faster in the long run, but he wanted to just run the 1500 to see if he could break the four-minute barrier.

He knew that the team needed the points he would score in the 800, but he really didn't like having to run it.

He won the 800 with ease, but he was trying to save his energy for his second race, the 1500. This being the first meet of the year, he had no clue what his time would be. He was hoping to break 4:10, but he wasn't sure he could pull it off this early in the season.

He had decided to do what he did in the NCAAs last year and start his kick going into the first turn of the last lap, instead of waiting until he came out of the second turn as he had always done in the past. He wasn't sure this strategy would work, and it would sure be embarrassing to get beat in his first race of the year.

Boots took the lead from the start and was never challenged. The question was, What was his winning time?

When the announcer came over the loud speaker and announced the order of finish, he read from fifth place forward.

"In first place is Boots Harris with a time of 4:05.2."

The stands went wild, and Boots put his hand on top of his head, realizing he was so close to breaking the four-minute barrier. He knew he could have run harder at the end. He also knew he could do it if he continued training like he had been and ran a smart race. He couldn't wait until next Saturday for the next meet.

Boots won the next three meets easily, but his times were not as good as the first meet. He couldn't figure out what was going wrong. It seemed like he was training harder and he was running harder in the races, but his times weren't as good.

Then next Saturday would be the last meet before the SEC meet. This was going to be a big meet with some of the best track-and-field teams in the eastern United States competing. This would be Boots's stiffest test to date, maybe even harder than the upcoming SEC championships.

Boots asked Coach Sines if he could not run in the 800 and just run the 1500. Since team points were not as important in this meet, the coach agreed.

Teams had certain uniforms they wore for the meets. They all had the same uniforms, warm-ups and so forth. Today as Boots walked to the starting line, he was wearing over his track uniform a Tennessee shirt. It was a special shirt, the one his mother had worn when she saw him run the only race she ever saw, the NCAA championships.

As runners were being announced over the loud speaker, he took the shirt off, folded it up neatly, and handed it to Coach Turner.

The starter announced for runners to take their marks.

Since this was such a large meet, there were a lot of runners in this race. Boots would have to be careful, especially at the start, to keep from getting bumped and maybe tripping over someone else.

The gun sounded, and off they went into the first turn. In big track meets like this one, there were usually runners called "rabbits" who would go out and set a very fast pace, trying to get other runners to go out too fast with them, and then they would be too tired to finish strong. Boots knew this, but at the same time, he hadn't run against most of the runners in the field, so he had to be careful and not get too far behind in case one of these runners was not a rabbit but just a very good runner.

After the first lap, Boots was in seventh place. He hoped that at least two of the runners ahead of him were rabbits, since they were setting such a fast pace.

Beginning the second lap, one of the rabbits dropped off of the track. He had passed a couple of the runners, so he was now in fourth place.

When the fourth lap began, Boots was in second place, and as he had done all year, he started his kick entering the first turn.

Boots had never been one to look over his shoulder at the finish, like a lot of runners did. He put his head down and ran as hard as he could, and when he reached the finish line, he leaned forward as far as he could without falling over.

He had won; he didn't know by how much, but he knew he had won. He was later told he won by seven yards. But what was his time? he wondered. It would be announced officially when they announced the order of finish.

He had walked almost a complete lap on the track to cool down before he heard the results.

As usual, the announcer started with fifth place and moved to first.

"First place from the University of Tennessee is Boots Harris with a new meet record of 3:58.7." A roar went up all around the track. Boots dropped to his knees in the third turn and put his hands over his eyes and began to cry. Teammates and runners from other schools ran to him and began to hug and slap him on the back, cheering for him.

Boots had to be helped to his feet, and a couple of his teammates grabbed him by the arms and made him jog in front of a cheering and screaming grandstand.

The cheering continued until the announcer told the fans that they needed to start the next race. It was still delayed another ten minutes before they became quiet enough to start the race.

As he walked over to the team area, Coach Turner handed him his mother's shirt and said, "Your parents are looking down from heaven, and they are proud. You are now a world-class athlete."

Boots put the shirt over his face and began to cry again.

He was now the odds-on favorite in the upcoming SEC championship. He was the favorite before, but this time was by far better than anyone else in the SEC.

The following week, he defended his 1500-meter championship. This time, he wore the Tennessee shirt that his father had worn in Texas. His time was 3:56.3. He was heading back to the NCAAs. This time, they would be held in Edwards Stadium in Berkeley, California. He was thrilled until he realized they would have to fly to California. He asked the coach to not put him near a window seat.

There were eight people who qualified from Tennessee for the NCAAs, twice as many as last year. Boots would be the favorite in the 1500, since he finished third last year and the top two runners from a year ago had graduated. There were several runners in the field who had faster times than last year's winner, but so did Boots.

The flight out was long and tiresome. Thanks goodness the coaches had enough sense to go out earlier than required to let the athletes' bodies adjust to the flight. Another thing Boots had trouble adjusting to was the time change. The weather there was hot, just like at home in Mississippi, but he hadn't trained there in years.

One thing Boots was not expecting was all the press coverage he was receiving. He could hardly get his workouts completed without someone shoving a microphone or camera in his face. He remembered Coach Turner's warning; the more well-known he got, the more people would want to be a part of his life. These people didn't seem like leeches though; they all seemed friendly and sincere.

When he had been in Austin, Texas, the year before, he had never seen a city so big. Now that he was in Berkeley, it was like he was on a different planet. He was an old country boy from Mississippi. He didn't understand most of what the people here were saying, and he had never seen people dress the way they did here. He had never seen so many roads and cars in his entire life. He remembered he still had never driven a car and still didn't have a driver's licenses. He knew he probably needed to learn to drive before he graduated college, but he didn't know anyone who had a car that would let him borrow it to learn to drive.

The big day arrived, race day. When big meets occurred, Boots wanted to be by himself and not talk to anyone. He needed to get psyched for the race. Today, he would wear both Tennessee shirts, his father's and mother's.

As with all big championships, the race was a dogfight. There were rabbits in these races too, but here, they usually weren't trying to help a teammate; they were runners who didn't have a good finishing kick, so they tried to set such as fast pace that the runners who did have a good kick would wear themselves out before the final lap and have no kick left. This was their only chance of winning.

The starter commanded the runners to take their marks.

Boots looked up to the heavens as if he was looking at his parents, hopeful God was taking time from his busy schedule to look down too.

The command came, "Set," and then the gun fired.

Boots sprinted faster than normal to the first turn. He hoped this wouldn't cost him at the end, but he didn't want to get boxed in by other runners.

Obviously, runners in the inside lane run a shorter distance than runners in the outer lanes. But to pass, you usually have to move out a lane or two. Boots didn't want to go out too far, but going into the third turn of the first lap, he found himself in the third lane. The two inside lanes were taken; he couldn't move in.

The first-place runner had a full five-yard lead over the entire field. Boots was banking on him having gone out too fast and fading later in the race.

Crossing the start-finish line after the first lap, Boots was in ninth place, way too far back. He was still in the third lane, which meant he was running much farther than the inside runner, but he couldn't get inside.

As they started down the backstretch of the second lap, he knew he had to get to the inside, but he would have to run faster than he had planned to do that. He didn't see any other way, so he took off.

He finally found an opening and moved to the inside lane; he was now in fifth, coming around to complete the second lap.

By the end of the third lap, he had moved up to fourth. He usually started his kick going into the first turn; he decided to start as soon as he crossed the finish line starting his final lap. He had never started that early before, but he felt he had to do it.

Coming down the final homestretch, there were three runners neck and neck. He closed his eyes and sprinted as hard as he could. He opened his eyes right before the finish line and leaned forward as far as he could; he lost his balance and fell face-first on the track.

He lay there for several seconds; he was so exhausted he couldn't get up. Some of the track officials helped him to his feet.

Boots asked them who won; no one knew.

There were cameras at the finish line, but it still took twenty minutes before they could decide who the winner was. Boots finished second; the race was so close that they awarded both runners the same time; 3:57.3.

At the start of the season, Boots wanted to repeat as SEC champ and break the four-minute barrier. He had broken it by more than almost three seconds. Boots truly had become world-class.

When they got back to the University of Tennessee and were making plans for Boots's senior year, Coach Sines said to Boots, "You have won the SEC two years in a row and will probably repeat this year, barring injury. You finished in third at the NCAAs your sophomore year and came within a hair of winning this year, and you will be favored heading into them this year. What a career. If you never win another race, you will go down as one of the best runners at UT and in the SEC, but I don't want that."

Boots looked at the coach strangely. *Isn't he satisfied with what I have accomplished?* Boots thought.

"You're coming up on your senior year, and you've had a great career, but I want more."

Boots again looked puzzled.

"Do you realize that the Summer Olympics occur in 1960?" the coach asked.

Boots had never even considered the possibility of making the Olympic team.

Coach Sines looked dead into his eyes and said, "You can do this if you want it bad enough."

Boots went back to his dorm. He walked in as his roommate was going to the cafeteria to eat. He was asked if he wanted to go eat, but he said, "No, I'll catch you there later."

"Is something wrong?" his roommate asked.

"They're talking about me trying for the Olympic team. Can you believe that?" Boots asked.

"Yes, I can believe that. Go for it. But I want an autographed picture." He laughed as he walked out the door.

This was the first time Boots had walked into the cafeteria since getting back from California. As he walked in, people started cheering and clapping. He turned red; he was embarrassed.

He got his meal, and people everywhere were inviting him to sit down and eat with them. He saw some of his teammates sitting at a table. He thanked the ones who wanted him to eat with them and said he needed to eat with his teammates. *They don't look like leeches*, he thought.

Boots had trouble sleeping that night. He was proud of all his accomplishments, but he had never thought he could reach the level where he would even be considered good enough to try out for the

Olympic team. He thought back to the day when he was getting ready to run the 100-yard dash in the eighth grade, and Coach Richards started calling him Boots.

As he lay there, he thought about being the first and only one in the family who had graduated from high school, and now it looked like he was going to graduate college. He wished his parents could see what he had accomplished after they died.

He finally drifted off to sleep, but he had dreams all night of crossing the finish line as an Olympic champion.

The following morning before going to class, he stopped by his mailbox and found a letter from Mr. Longhurst. In the letter, he told him how proud he was of him. At the end of the letter, he said he hoped he would be around to see him win the NCAAs next year; he was dying of cancer.

Boots was shocked. Even though Mr. Longhurst had been his parents' employer for all their lives and he had worked for him too, he had always treated him like a friend rather than a boss. He thought about praying to God to help cure his cancer, but he remembered that God only answered prayers of his children. He would ask Coach Turner to add him to the prayer list at church. He knew he needed to accept God so he could be in heaven with his mother and father but just not right now.

Boots had to make a decision. Should he take a job and try to make some of the money back he had to spend for his mother's funeral, or should he go to summer school and try to finish college early and start training for a chance at making the Olympic team? He decided to talk to his coach, friend, and pastor.

He told Coach Turner about the conversation he had with Coach Sines about the Olympics.

Coach Turner said, "Yes, Coach Sines and I have talked about it a lot. Being an SEC champion is something, and being an NCAA champion is something, but being able to say you were on the US

Olympic team is something not many people get a chance to do. Even if you finish last place, you can still say, 'I'm an Olympian,' and that means a lot. I know SEC champions and NCAA champions, but I don't know an Olympian.

"Coach Sines and I have talked about this for some time. If you decide to do this, cross-country meets, track meets, SEC championships, NCAA championships mean nothing; we will be training you to make the Olympic team—period."

Boots didn't know what to think. He had just heard about the Olympics, but it seemed that the coaches had been talking about it for some time.

He liked being the two-time SEC champion and the NCAA runner-up by a hair. People looked up to him and wanted to know him. He had seen no leeches trying to use him. He remembered being a nobody in middle school, and he wasn't sure he wanted to give this fame up.

What if he tried to make the Olympic team and in the process lost his SEC title, and since he would probably be favored in the NCAA 1500 next year, what if he flopped there too? Then all he had accomplished to this point would be forgotten. He had to think about this long and hard before he decided what to do.

In the meantime, he was being asked to attend a lot of parties. He had never been on a date in his life, but a lot of girls were asking him to go with him to certain parties. He didn't see anything wrong with accepting some of them. They weren't leeches, just normal students. Being a champion should make people want to know you. He was watching for the leeches that Pastor Turner had warned him about, but he hadn't run into them yet.

Boots decided to attend summer school, which would enable him to graduate in the spring. He would be able to train for the Olympics, and if it didn't work out, he would still graduate at the end of the semester next spring.

He went to tell Coach Sines he had decided to try to make the Olympic team. He didn't like what he heard.

The coach told him if he wanted to try to make the Olympic team, he needed to give up the 800 meters, which made Boots smile, but he needed to add the 3200 meters to build up his endurance.

Boots had never run a 3200-meter race. He didn't like the coach's idea.

"As a matter of fact, in some of the smaller meets, I want you to run all three—the 800, 1500, and the 3200. That will help you billed up your speed and endurance."

When Boots heard that, he wished he had never even brought it up. How could he run three races a meet and be able to win all of them?

Coach Sines seem to read Boots's mind. "If we are training for the Olympics, we forget about wins and losses in races; we concentrate on one goal—the Olympic trials and making the team. You have to forget about your pride—'Well, I'm the defending SEC champion; I should be the NCAA champion this year.' All that doesn't matter. We have one goal and one goal only. Do you understand?"

Boots didn't understand; it seemed like a lot to be giving up for a chance at something that seemed so remote a possibility, but he nodded his head yes anyway.

He went back to his room confused. Why should be blow his senior year, with all the races and championships he could win, for a chance that seemed impossible to achieve? All track athletes had Olympic dreams, and very few had any real possibility of reaching them. How was he any different?

Once again, he couldn't sleep that night, thinking of what to do. He decided to talk to Coach Turner tomorrow; he knew he would give him a straight answer.

The following day, he went by Coach Turner's office, and the secretary said he had gone to a religious conference and would not be back until the end of the week.

Boots didn't know who to talk to, and then he remembered that Mr. Longhurst had given him his phone number and told him to call if he needed to talk. He wasn't sure he should call, knowing that he had cancer. He wasn't even sure if he was out of the hospital.

Boots knew the call would be expensive, but he needed the advice of someone he could trust. He went to a pay phone and dialed the number.

It was several seconds before someone answered the phone. He asked to speak to Mr. Longhurst.

"He's resting right now. Can I ask who's calling?"

Boots told her his name.

She said she would pass on the message, and he would get back to him.

Boots said, "You don't understand. I have no phone, and I'm calling from a pay phone. Mr. Longhurst gave me his number and said to call him if I needed anything. I need to talk to him; he can't call me back. This is a pay phone."

"Just a minute. I'll see if he will talk to you."

Boots waited for several minutes. The phone kept asking for more quarters, and he didn't have many left.

Finally, Mr. Longhurst came on the line.

Boots explained the situation about the Olympics and asked what he thought he should do.

Mr. Longhurst said, "Who remembers an SEC champion five years later? Who remembers the NCAA champion ten years later? I can tell you—only their friends and family. If you make the Olympic team, you are always remembered. Go for it."

Boots decided not to wait until Coach Turner returned; he told Coach Sines the next day that he was in. "Olympics all the way," Boots said. "Go, Big Orange."

"Great. I'm for the Tennessee track team all the way, as I have been since I was hired. But potential Olympic athletes don't come along very often. I not only think you can make the Olympic team, but I think you can win the Olympics. We are not just going to train you to get a US Olympic uniform and march in the opening ceremonies; we are going to train you to win. So, if your goals are lower than that, we are wasting our time; we'll just shoot for the SEC and NCAAs. So, we are in it to win it all, or we aren't in it at all. What's your decision?"

Boots sat there for a few minutes, thinking over what he had just heard. He was already an SEC champion and almost an NCAA champion, but he wanted it all. He had been a nobody long enough; he wanted to be a somebody.

"Let's go for the gold," he told Coach Sines.

"We start training tomorrow, Olympic champion," Coach said. He reached out and shook Boots's hand.

"We are now on a mission," Coach said.

The coaches sat down and planned his training for the next year, even down to what he should and shouldn't eat. If a meet conflicted with his training program, he would just not run the meet.

Coach Sines had been around track all of his life and knew a lot of present and former world-class runners. Of the ones who were no longer running, he contacted many of them and asked for advice. The ones who were still competing, he studied how they trained.

Coach Sines told Boots he had two days off, and then the training would begin. "You better enjoy the two days because it will probably the last ones you get for a long time," Coach Sines said.

Coach Turner was assigned to be his full-time trainer. His duties as assistant track coach would be handled by graduate assistants.

Boots was put through all kinds of training. When he was taken out to a part of the campus that had a slight downhill grade and was told he was going to run sprints downhill, Boots asked why he couldn't just do them on a track like normal.

Coach Turner explained that this was a new technique that Coach Sines had come up with. By sprinting downhill, the incline would make the legs move faster than they could on a flat surface; therefore, he would be building up sprinting muscles beyond their normal range.

"Does this really work?" Boots asked.

"I guess we will find out. Coach Sines seems to think it will."

Another thing that changed was that Boots was supposed to go to the training room after every workout and receive leg massages to get the soreness and fatigue out of his legs. Coach Turner began to learn how to do the massages for the times the trainers were not available.

The swimming pool was used a lot for running after several days of heavy workouts.

He was to be in bed no later than ten thirty each night.

Many days, he was required to run two hard workouts in the same day, one early in the morning and the other late. Days when the temperature was nearing a hundred degrees, he would run in the hottest part of the day. They practiced in all weather conditions since they had no idea what weather conditions would be present the days he would have to run in Rome.

Boots's class load was cut in half, just enough courses to keep him eligible to run in college.

Later in the winter when the cold and flu season hit the campus hard, his professors granted him permission to be tutored away from class so he would not catch anything from the other students and have to miss training.

As the fall semester began, he would compete in only two of the seven scheduled cross-country meets. The coaches wanted him to run only on the flatter courses. In the two meets he ran in, he blew the field away.

He asked if he could run in the SEC cross-country championships but was told no.

Boots ran every day, even on Christmas. He ate Christmas dinner at Coach Turner's house, but his food was monitored. He was allowed only a small piece of pie.

The days it snowed, he ran in the field house. If snow presided for several days, he was loaded into the van and driven across the state line to South Carolina or Georgia so he could still get in the workouts he needed.

As track season rolled around, he ran only certain meets. In some meets, he ran the 800 and the 1500 meters. Other meets, he might run the 1500 and 3200 meters. He won every race going away. He lowered his 1500-meter time to 3:49, more than ten seconds better than his best time last year.

With the SEC meet coming up, Coach Sines wasn't sure he was going to let Boots run. Boots kept begging until the coach finally agreed. But he told him they would treat it like a workout, and winning was not their goal. That's what Boots was told, but he had no intention of losing the SEC his senior year. He won by fifteen yards, with a time of 3:46.7.

The NCAAs would be held in Berkeley, California, which meant they would have to fly there; Boots was not looking forward to the flight after his last experience on an airplane.

The coaches were eager for Boots to run and train in California, as they expected this climate to be similar to the conditions he would face in Rome.

So many runners had made the qualifying time for the 1500 meters that there would be two qualifying races to see who would be in the finals. The twelve who had the fastest times would be in the finals; where one placed in the heat race made no difference. Therefore, Boots would have to run two hard races in two days.

He wore his mother's and father's Tennessee shirts over his uniform once again, but this time he had to take them off before going onto the track, as Coach Turner was not allowed on the track in this big competition.

Boots won his heat with a time of 3:47, which was slower than his last race, but he only wanted to qualify for the final and not go all out.

Boots had already made the qualifying time and been invited to the Olympic trials next month, but he really wanted to win the NCCA 1500-meter championship. A lot of things could go wrong before Rome, so he didn't want to blow this chance at being a champion. The trials would be held in Stanford Stadium in California, which mean another long plane flight.

The finals of the 1500 were run at seven o'clock the following day. When Boots woke up and looked outside, it was raining. He never liked to run in the rain, but he didn't know of many runners who did, so it would be the same for everyone.

As he started to walk on the track, he took his parents' Tennessee shirts off and handed them to Coach Turner. They looked into each other's eyes, and Coach Turner said, "You can do this. Be smart and don't get boxed in."

Usually in big races like this, every runner thought they were good enough to at least win a medal, so there were not as many rabbits in a race like this. Plus, a rabbit usually had a teammate in the race that he was trying to help win, and in this race, it was every man for his self.

The race was surprisingly easy for Boots. He was in third place after the first two laps and then moved up to take the lead on the third and never looked back. His winning time was 3:47.4, a new meet record.

As he climbed to the top of the awards stand to receive his medal, he was wearing his parents' Tennessee shirts again.

Boots would now have a little over a month before he would be flying back to California for the Olympic trials. As they were boarding the plane, he turned and looked over his shoulder, hoping that the next time he was boarding a plane to fly back to Tennessee, he would be a part of the US Olympic team.

As he sat down in his aisle seat as far away from the windows as he could get, Coach Sines told him he could take today and tomorrow off and rest his body. He couldn't remember the last time he had a day off, much less two. He had not been looking forward to having to train today after the long flight across the US.

While Boots was sleeping on the flight home, the coaches were mapping out his training schedule before the Olympic trials next month. He seemed to be right on schedule; his times had been going down, and he was learning how to handle different situations that cropped up during races. From here on out, a mistake in a race would mean he was going back home.

Once again, after getting back to school, he was even more popular than he had ever been. Students flocked around him everywhere he went. Everyone wanted to sit next to him in the lunchroom. Radio and TV stations wanted him for interviews. Sports reporters wanted to write stories about him in their newspapers. He was continually asked to attend parties and functions. He politely turned down all the parties and functions, explaining he was still in training, but he couldn't very well turn down members of the press. At least classes were over now, and he had a little more free time.

A month before the trials, he walked into Coach Sines's office and told the coach he felt like he was coming down with something. He was immediately taken to the doctors who worked with the athletes at UT and given a complete physical. It was determined that he had allergies, so he was given some medicine to take and sent back out to train.

When word got around town that the track team went over their budget, mainly because of added expenses of trying to get Boots to Rome, several influential businessmen stepped forward with the funds to provide for not only the needed trip to California but also money to put Boots and the coaches in one of the quality hotels in California. Several of these men offered their private plane to transport the trio to California and back.

As they boarded the private plane, Coach Turner asked Boots if he had his parents' Tennessee shirts, and he told him that was the first thing he had packed.

Before leaving, Boots had received a letter from Mr. Longhurst telling him that he and his wife would be in the stands cheering him on.

Boots knew that Mr. Longhurst was someone special; not many men who were wealthy enough to own a plantation would take the time out to care about someone who used to pick cotton for him.

The flight was a lot quicker than flying commercial flights. There were no layovers or delays; they only landed to refuel. The downside was there were no aisle seats to sit in; unless he stared straight ahead the whole flight, Boots would have to look out at the land far below. He couldn't imagine the flight he would have to take to Rome if he was lucky enough to make the team.

Instead of getting rooms at one of the expensive hotels, Coach Sines had studied the area around the stadium where the trials were to be held and contacted one of the smaller colleges. He made arrangements with them to let Boots use their track to train on, and he also wanted an area where they could train that had hills or mountains. They stayed in a motel near Foothill College, five miles from the center of Stanford University.

After Boots had a four-mile, slow jog, they drove over in a rented car to see the track at Stanford. Boots knew his dreams would either come true here in a few days or be shattered.

As with the NCAAs, there would be several heats, with the fastest times qualifying for the finals the following Saturday.

The coaches knew it was important to keep Boots on easy workouts the next several days. They wanted his legs to be fresh and rested, not sore and tired. Some runners trained so hard right up until the race that their bodies couldn't perform well in the race.

One of Coach Sines's requirements for his athletes had always been that they attend worship service on Sunday; this Sunday was no exception. They found a local church and attended services just like always.

The following day, trials began for all the different track-and-field events. After Boots's morning workout, they went to the stadium and sat in the stands and watched some of the events being held.

Boots didn't know that Coach Sines was supposed to be in Atlanta, Georgia, that night to receive a coach of the year award from the *Atlanta Journal-Constitution* newspaper. He was voted the SEC for track-and-field coach of the year.

Coach Sines told them to mail the plaque to his office at the University of Tennessee; he was going to be getting his runner qualified to run in the Olympics. Seems no one had thought about a coach being at the Olympic trials the same day.

The day of his first qualifying race came. He would have to run on Tuesday and Thursday, hoping to make it to the finals on Saturday.

He had meet with Mr. Longhurst and his wife, along with the owner of the plane they flew out on and other big businessmen who had provided money for the trip.

Boots did his usual prerace stretching and loosening up. He felt good but very nervous. He had never seen this many track fans or faced this stiff of competition. There were runners in every heat capable of winning in the finals of the 1500.

The plan was for Boots to run as slow of a time as he could yet make it to the next heat on Thursday. He needed to conserve as much energy as he could for the finals on Saturday.

Boots finished second in his first qualifying heat. He felt he could have won if he wanted to, but advance and move on was the goal. His time was 3:42 even, his fastest time ever.

The following day was just a slow, light workout day. Coach Turner gave Boots's legs a good massage to work the soreness and fatigue out.

They went and ate a good meal, then went back to the hotel and got Boots off of his feet as much as possible. Some reporters wanted to interview Coach Sines in the lobby, so Boots and Coach Turner were in the room alone.

Coach Turner once again told Boots that if he made the US Olympic team, people would be crawling out of the woodwork to get close to him. Most of these people where great people and only wanted the best for him, but there would be another set of people who wanted to use him to better themselves.

Coach also reminded Boots that all this popularity was just a moment in time, and what he needed to worry about was coming to know the Lord and worry about the eternal rewards of heaven.

Boots started to say something, but Coach Sines walked back into the room, so he just kept quiet. He had already seen how people were being drawn to him the more races he won and the more his name was in the paper. He also knew that what the coach was saying about God was true, but he needed to worry about making the team right now; he could worry about the God stuff later.

The following day, they didn't even go to the stadium. They ate breakfast and later all just took a long walk together. When they got back to the hotel, Boots spent about twenty minutes stretching, and then Coach Turner massaged his legs, and he lay in bed watching TV most of the afternoon.

They arrived at the track about two hours before his race. As before all races, he spent a lot of time stretching. If he felt any tightness in his legs, Coach Turner would try to work it out with a massage.

When he walked onto the track, he was wearing his parents' Tennessee shirts. The runners would be introduced over the loud speaker and then would take their warm-ups or any clothing they were not going to wear during the race and hand them to the helpers who were working at the track. When he handed the two shirts to the worker, he pointed to Coach Sines standing near the fence and told them to make sure he gave the shirts to the coach standing over there in orange.

Like the previous race, Boots jumped out near the front to avoid any chance of being tripped up in the start. He stayed near the front until the last lap and then pulled away to win by a couple of yards; his time was 3:41.9, his fastest ever. When he heard his time announced, he was surprised that it was that fast. It had not seemed like this was his fastest race ever. He was now in the finals on Saturday night. If he could finish in the top three, he would make the Olympic team. *Two down and one to go*, he thought.

He walked over to the fence, and Coach Sines handed him the Tennessee shirts. He put them on and began walking by himself to cool down.

Coach Sines was sitting in the stands with his Tennessee coaching shirt on when the lady sitting behind him asked him why the Tennessee runner wore two shirts over his uniform when it was so hot.

Coach Sines told her about Boots's parents and the shirts. She began to cry.

Saturday seemed to be so slow in coming to Boots and the coaches. This was the day they all had been working toward for the last year.

The field was composed of the twelve best 1500-meter runners in the history of US track. If Boots could finish in the top three, he would make the team. He was always nervous before a race, but he had never felt this nervous. It seemed like everyone was counting on him, and he didn't want to let anyone down.

The race began with a lot of pushing and shoving; two runners fell going into the first turn. He needed to keep his composure after he almost fell over one of the runners that were down.

Boots began to think something was wrong; he just didn't feel normal. He couldn't put his finger on what was wrong, but he had never felt so uncomfortable running a race before.

He was in fifth place after two laps; he needed to be in the top three.

Coming up on the third lap, Boots had move up into third; if he could just maintain that position.

Up until this year, Boots had always waited until he started coming off the second turn to start his kick. This year, he had changed and started his kick going into the first turn on the last lap, and it had worked for him all year. Now he was questioning himself about waiting until the second turn again.

He was in third place, and all he needed to do was hold that position to make the team. He decided to wait until the second turn to start his kick.

As they were entering the second turn, he saw two runners moving up on his outside. Had he waited too long? he asked himself.

He began his kick down the backstretch. He went back ahead of the two runners who had pulled up alongside him.

Coming out of the fourth turn, he was in the third lane a few yards behind the first and second runners, but he sensed runners approaching over his shoulder.

The last thing Boots remembered before leaning at the finish line was there were several runners on both sides of him leaning also. After he crossed the line, he looked up at the scoreboard to see where he had finished. *Just please let me have made the team God*, he thought.

Several minutes passed, but there were still no results on the board. They finally put up fifth through last, but the first four were blank. Every runner and everyone in the stands was looking at the board.

Boots rolled over on his side to look at the scoreboard, but he was having trouble seeing; he was getting dizzy.

Finally Boots looked to the stands where his coaches were sitting, trying to get a sign, when he heard a loud roar. He turned to look at the giant scoreboard.

Boots put his hands over his face and began to cry; he had won. His time was 3:41.6, a new meet record, and he was no longer a fast 1500-meter runner; he had stepped up to now be a world-class 1500-meter runner.

His competitors huddle around him, patting him on the back.

Someone handed one of the other runners who had qualified an American flag, and the three who had made the team jogged around the track arm in arm, waving the flag. Boots could not stop crying.

As he walked out the gate separating the track from the stands, he was mobbed by his coaches, boosters, Mr. Longhurst, and people he didn't even know.

After the initial commotion died down, Mr. Longhurst asked if he could take him and the coaches out to eat.

Boots said he would ask the coaches. They agreed but said it would probably be late because he had a lot of interviews to do before they could eat.

Boots told Mr. Longhurst it was all right with the coaches, but it would probably be a while before they could go.

Mr. Longhurst said, "Boots, I'm going to buy you the biggest steak in California."

Boots thanked him but didn't tell him he had never eaten a steak; he had grown up eating bologna and spam as his meats. On special occasions like Thanksgiving and Christmas, they had a chicken but never steak.

Boots lost count of how many microphones had been shoved in front of his face. He lost count of TV interviews too. The coach finally stopped all interviews and said, "We don't want to be rude, but this kid has not eaten since eleven this morning. He needs food."

Mr. Longhurst picked up Boots and the coaches and took them to a restaurant that none of them had heard of. They were told to order anything on the menu. It was on him.

Boots had eaten hamburgers before, but he wasn't sure about the steak. What if he ordered it and didn't like it?

Mr. Longhurst pointed at the menu and said to Boots, "See that steak right there? That will be the best steak you have ever put in your mouth."

Boots didn't tell him he had never put a steak in his mouth before; he went ahead and ordered it.

When the waiter asked him what salad dressing he wanted on his salad, he had no clue what to say. He had eaten some salads in the school cafeteria, but he didn't know the name of the dressings he had put on them. He asked Mr. Longhurst what he suggested, and he said thousand island, so that's what he got. He couldn't figure out why they would name a salad dressing after islands somewhere.

When Boots tasted the steak, he thought he had died and gone to heaven. It was the best thing he had ever tasted. While eating, he thought, *I need to make a decision about this heaven stuff but not tonight.*

When they got back to the hotel, everyone was so hyped up, and nobody could sleep. They kept replaying the race over and over. They turned on the different TV stations and saw the finish and some of the interviews Boots had done.

When Boots saw the finish on television, he could see why it took so long to determine the finish. It looked like everyone crossed the finish line at the same time.

When they went down for breakfast the following morning, there were reporters standing there waiting on them. There was even a reporter from the Knoxville station who had flown in overnight to get an interview.

The flight home was on the private plane that had flown them out to California, but this time the owner of the plane wanted to fly back with the coaches and Boots. *Friend or leech?* Boots thought.

Upon arriving back in Knoxville, there was what seemed like thousands of people waiting for the plane to land. As Boots climbed out of the plane, students and people were cheering everywhere. Many had made large signs congratulating Boots on his win. There were a lot of Go Vols signs.

There were lots of reporters from radio and TV there to interview him. They decided to go into the airport and use a special room that the airport had set up for all the interviews.

They arrived at two in the afternoon, but it was almost four thirty before they were finished and ready to leave.

The following morning when Boots walked into the cafeteria for breakfast, the entire cafeteria stood up and began cheering. Even the cafeteria staff was cheering.

Everyone wanted to pat him on the back or just be around him. Everyone wanted him to sit down and eat with them. It took him an hour to eat instead of the normal fifteen minutes.

Since he was not in school during the summer, he didn't have to go to class or work at his library job. He just needed to eat and do his workouts, and he was free the rest of the day.

He was handed all kinds of notes during lunch, inviting him to parties and from girls with their phone numbers on the paper. *Leeches*, he thought.

Even though it was the last of July and very hot, he decided to put his hooded sweatshirt on, and he wore dark glasses to avoid all the attention he was getting.

When he was out on long runs away from campus, people would honk their horns and roll their windows down and want to talk to him. If he slowed down to talk, he wasn't getting the training in he needed. If he just waved and ignored the people, they thought he was a snob and gave him the finger.

The 1500-meter heats would begin on September 3 in Rome, so he would have a little over a month to prepare. The coaches had decided to go over two weeks in advance to get used to the climate and surroundings.

The commotion caused by Boots winning was affecting their ability to train and work with him, so the coaches decided to travel to another unknown state and train before they left for Rome. No one was told their location, not even the coach's families. They were afraid someone would accidentally let it slip where they were.

The Olympic Committee sent a letter requesting Boots's measurements for the clothes he would be wearing during the opening ceremonies and his running gear.

Two days before leaving for Rome, they returned to the university to gather their things that they were going to take with them to Rome and say goodbye to their families. Boots still couldn't believe he was going to the Olympics.

There was a huge crowd at the send-off. It would take them two days to reach Rome because of a few layovers. Boots still didn't like to fly, but there was no other way to get there on time. Once again, Boots chose the aisle seat.

After a long trip over and having to deal with the time change, they decided to take a nap after arriving at their hotel. Boots had planned on doing a light workout, but his legs felt like lead from the long plane ride.

They were there for one reason—to win. But Boots picked up some of the travel brochures in the lobby to see what was near them; maybe they could see a few things between workouts. It would be up to Coach Sines.

They had received the schedule for everything from the opening ceremonies to the closing ones. Since Boots had several days between the opening ceremonies and when he was supposed to run his first heat, he felt sure Coach would allow him to march in it.

He had never seen the Olympics on TV before, but he had gone to a movie theater once, and it had shown the US team marching into the stadium with their uniforms on. He wished his parents could witness it. He hoped they were looking down from heaven and could see it. He still had to decide about this heaven stuff, but right now he needed to worry about the race.

Since most of the athletes and coaches were staying in dorms that had been built for the Olympics, they did not have to rent a car or van. A shuttle bus was constantly running back and forth from the dorms to the stadium.

There was also a practice track for the athletes to use away from the main stadium. The problem was there were so many athletes there it was always full.

That night after eating and before he went to his dorm room, Coach Turner handed Boots a small package. It had been sent to the coach's office before they left. Coach Turner had packed it but had forgotten to give it to Boots on the flight over; it was from Mr. Longhurst.

"What is it?" Boots asked.

"I have no clue. Open it and find out."

Boots opened it to find a camera with a note attached to it.

The note simply said, "Win and take a lot of pictures. This is a once-in-a-lifetime experience that few get to experience."

"I don't even know how to use a camera," Boots said.

Coach Turner showed him how to use it.

"You can carry it with you in the opening ceremonies and take pictures of everything going on," the coach said.

Even though Boots's first race was more than two weeks off, the opening ceremonies were in three days.

When he got back to his dorm, he saw a package lying on his bed with his name on it. He opened it up, and inside was his uniform and the clothes he was to wear during the opening ceremonies.

He saw an identical package lying on the other bed. He had been told he would share a room, but he didn't know who with. He walked over and read the name on the box—Jim Maci.

Jim had been the runner who was awarded third place in the close finish at the Olympic trials. Boots didn't know much about him; they had only spoken a few times.

Boots decided to try on his track uniform first. He felt a lump in his throat when he looked in the mirror and saw the USA emblem on the front.

He then decided to try on the uniform they were to wear in the opening ceremonies. There was even a funny-looking straw hat with a red, white, and blue ribbon around it.

As he was looking at himself in the mirror, with the ridiculous-looking hat on, he heard someone putting a key in the door, and before he knew it, in walked Jim Maci.

"Are you going to a costume party?" Jim laughed.

"Don't laugh. You've got this clown suit too," Boots replied. "Have you ever seen such a stupid hat?"

"Yes, but I know a lot of athletes still at home who would love to be wearing it," Jim said.

The two shook hands and congratulated each other for making the team.

Jim saw the camera lying on the dresser and said, "Let me take your picture."

Boots really didn't want his picture taken in this outfit, but he didn't want to be rude. He told Jim he would just hold the hat by his side instead of wearing it.

"I don't blame you." Jim laughed.

After he stored his things away, he asked, "Is there anywhere to eat around here? I'm starved."

"The cafeteria is right around the corner. I don't know how late they serve, but I'll walk there with you and see."

The cafeteria was still open. He was a little hungry even though he had eaten earlier, but he wasn't sure if he could eat again on his meal card, so he just sat down and talked to Jim while he ate.

He found out that Jim went to the University of Oregon and had just graduated.

Boots shared part of his story with Jim. He left out the part about growing up on a cotton plantation and about his parents both dying.

The following morning, each athlete met with their coaches to begin their final few days of training. Boots was so used to his workout schedule he could almost do it in his sleep. He had actually participated in very few competitions over the last year. His workouts had been geared for the following few races.

After the morning workout, Boots went to the cafeteria to eat. He saw Jim and sat down beside him. There were athletes from all over the world; so many languages were being spoken all over the cafeteria. Boots saw a couple of SEC runners from other schools who had made the team, and he gave them a friendly nod.

As he and Jim were talking, Bruce Michaels walked up and said hello and asked if he could join them. Bruce had finished second in the photo finish at the trials.

The three had a lot in common. They had all finally reached the dream of being a member of the US Olympic team, but they all had another dream in common—being the Olympic champion.

The three hung out together quite a bit over the next few days. They decided to walk together during the opening ceremonies.

Like in the past before big meets, Coach Sines had Boots perform very light workouts the days leading up to the first race; he wanted his legs to be fresh.

Athletes were able to watch all the pre-Olympic hype on the local television stations. Many athletes were interviewed prior to their races. Boots was asked but declined.

The US team gathered outside the stadium along with the other nations to begin their entrance into the stadium. Since nations marched in alphabetical order, the US was one of the last teams to enter the stadium. Boots could hear all the cheers as each nation was introduced. He had his camera with him, and he hoped he remembered how to use it.

Finally it was the United States' turn to enter the stadium. Boots was about halfway back in the pack of athletes. As he entered the stadium, he had never seen such a sight in his life. The stadium was packed, and people were cheering and screaming to the point it was almost deafening. He saw cameras flashing all around the stadium. There were TV cameras filming from all angles. The athletes were waving to the stands, and the stands were waving back to the athletes. Boots had never seen anything like it.

Boots reached into his pocket and pulled out the camera that Mr. Longhurst had sent him and started taking pictures. He was waving at people he had never seen before, and he was surrounded by some of the most famous athletes the United States had to offer. For a moment, he thought, *This must be what heaven is like.* He knew he had been putting it off, but he needed to make a decision as soon as these races were over.

After all the nations had been introduced, the announcer was saying things in English, and then they were being translated in another language that Boots had no clue what it was.

Finally, a big cheer went up as the Olympic torch entered the stadium. As the Olympic flame was lit, the announcer proclaimed the Olympic Games were beginning. Boots could hardly keep his heart in his chest. He had never experienced such a moment in his life.

That night after returning to the dorm, he and Jim talked about all that had gone on at the stadium. Boots knew he would have trouble going to sleep because of all that had happened. He still had not gotten used to the time difference between there and back in Tennessee.

The days seemed to pass extra slowly. Boots had been to the stadium to watch several races and performed his daily workouts, but he was ready for his races to begin.

Finally, the day of his first heat arrived. Even though he would run in his USA uniform, he wore the two Tennessee shirts over it up until the last minute.

Like the Olympic trials in the US, there would be two heats and then the finals. Unlike the US trials, there would be fifteen runners in each heat, as compared to twelve in the US trials. Once again, the finals would be according to times, not finishes in the heats.

Boots was second in his first heat race, with a time of 3:45.6. This was not a fast time, but he had finished second in his heat; he was going to have to do much better to have a chance for a medal. He would have a day off before his next heat.

To Boots's sorrow, it looked like Jim Maci had been eliminated; he had finished sixth in the heat. Bruce had finished fourth with a time that might hold up.

Two days later, Boots was running again. As it turned out, Bruce's time was not good enough to advance, so now Boots was the only American with a chance to make it into the finals.

Once again, Boots finished second in his heat, with a time of 3:44.6. He had made the finals, but he knew he would have to run much faster to have a chance to medal.

Coach Sines continued his belief in his training methods; he had Boots do mostly stretching, with a lot of deep leg massages the following day.

Boots spent a lot of his free time by himself thinking about his and his parents' life and how he had been the first to graduate high school and now he was almost ready to graduate college.

He reflected how he had a chance to make something of himself.

His parents had never owned a car, a TV, a phone, an electric stove, or a refrigerator. They had never even owned something as simple as a flashlight. He could finally break the poverty lifestyle that had plagued his family for generations.

He thought about how Coach Sines and Coach Turner had sacrificed time from their families and taken away times when they should have been working with the track and cross-country team to help him. He thought about all the individuals and fans at the University of Tennessee who had gone above and beyond to help get him in this position. He felt truly blessed, and he knew God was helping him; he would start accepting and working for God just as soon as this race was over.

The following day, the coaches discussed strategy with Boots. They went over each runner in the finals—their strengths and weaknesses.

They talked about when Boots should begin his kick. Most of the season, he had started heading into the first turn, but he had also reverted to years past when he waited until coming out of the second turn. They discussed which option he should use according to where he was going into the last lap and who might be ahead of him. They had studied this to the point there was nothing left to do but run the race.

Boots had trouble going to sleep. He still had not adjusted to this time change. Plus, it had rained all night. He sure didn't want to run in the rain. The forecast predicted a 50 percent chance of rain at the scheduled start of the race.

He decided to wear his parents' shirts all day. It was hard to get his mother's shirt on over his uniform because it was so small. He usually put his mother's shirt on first and then his father's on over the other two.

There would be no training or workout during the time leading up to the race, only stretching and leg massages.

It seemed like the day would never end. He tried to sleep, read, and watch TV, but nothing seemed to make the day go by faster.

Finally, the time had arrived. Runners were told to take their marks. Boots knew that even though it would take less than four minutes, these next few minutes would, to a large extent, determine his future.

The command "set" was given, and the gun was fired.

After the first lap, Boots was back in seventh place in a field of fifteen. Going into the second turn, the leader pulled a hamstring and limped off to the side. He was now in sixth, still too far back.

By the end of the second lap, he had dropped back to seventh. *What was going on?* he thought. He knew he should be closer to the front than this. In all the excitement, he had not heard the first two lap times; he didn't know that the pace was a lot faster than normal.

Coming out of the fourth turn of the third lap, a couple of runners had faded; he now was in fifth place. He had never started his kick before the first turn, but for some reason, he started as soon as he crossed the finish line of the last lap. He didn't think he would be able to maintain his finishing kick for a lap. He decided to go for broke; he was either going to medal or collapse before the finish. He figured if he wasn't in the top three for a medal, what difference did it make where he finished?

The last lap was a blur to Boots. All he knew was he was running as hard as he could, and when he heard the fans cheering, he knew he was near the finish. He ran five yards past the finish line before he knew the race was over. He fell on the track exhausted. He didn't know where he finished or what his time was; he just knew the race was over and he could breathe again.

He lay on the track exhausted. He could hear several runners saying, "Good race, man," but that was what everyone said after the race.

Boots was so tired he just wished everyone would leave him alone and just let him go to sleep right there on the track.

Several emergency personnel ran over to him to see if he was all right. They helped him to his feet and made him start walking to get his body back to functioning again.

One of the attendants said, "Let's go, man. Start walking. You've got to climb those steps in a minute."

Boots had no clue what he was talking about. He was so out of it he hardly knew where he was. He knew one thing: if he never ran another step, it would be too soon.

As they were in the second turn, Boots asked who won.

"What do you mean who won? You did," one of the emergency personnel said.

Boots looked up at the big scoreboard, and his name was in first with a time of 3:41.6. Boots fell to the track again in tears; he had done it. He was an Olympic champion.

He was helped to the backstretch by the emergency personnel until he could walk on his own. Someone handed him an American flag, which he draped around his shoulders, and someone else handed him a small flag on a stick. He walked around to the finish line, waving the American flag. His coaches were standing behind the fence at the finish line, and he walked over, and they all embraced with tears of joy running down their faces.

Coach Turner handed him his parents' Tennessee shirts, and he held one in each hand and waved to the crowd, who was cheering louder than he had ever heard before.

Later, he was standing atop the podium and received his medal. Standing on either side were the second- and third-place medalists. Michael Jazy from France finished second, and Iatvan Rozsavolgi from Hungry was third.

Boots bent down to have the gold medal placed around his neck. As he stood back up straight, he took the medal with his right hand and looked at it. His dream had finally come true. Just then, the United States national anthem began playing. He placed his hand over his heart and began to cry.

The rest of the week was a blur. He wore the medal everywhere he went, and people from countries all over the world came up and patted him on the back and congratulated him. Many were speaking to him in languages he couldn't understand. The reporters and press were asking for interviews everywhere he went. He lost count of how many TV and radio interviews he had done since the race was over.

He received letters and telegrams from home, including from Mr. Longhurst, friends, athletes, and coaches.

His former eighth grade coach, Coach Richards, had said in his telegram, "I guess this will start a trend of more future athletes starting their training wearing oversized boots. Congratulations. I'm proud of you."

Since they would be staying for the closing ceremonies, Boots got to enjoy the rest of the games from the stands. He didn't have to train every day anymore. He also could, for the first time in over a year, eat what he wanted. There were several meals in which all he ate was dessert.

At closing ceremonies, the United States team members were given a small American flag on a stick to wave. After they had marched around the track and were standing in their assigned area for the closing ceremonies, Boots took out his camera and used up the rest of the role of film he had in the camera. He had taken four roles of pictures with the camera that Mr. Longhurst had sent him. He had no clue how to get them developed; he would have to ask someone when he got home how to turn the little round things with film on them into pictures.

After the long flight home, he stepped out of the plane to walk down the steps, and he saw thousands of people cheering and screaming.

At the bottom of the steps, a microphone had been set up for him to be interviewed by radio and TV stations from all around. There were NBC and CBS cameras there as well stations he had never heard of.

In the final part of the ceremonies, the mayor presented Boots the keys to the city of Knoxville. Boots held up the keys in one hand and his gold medal in the other. A huge roar went up from the crowd.

When he finally reached his dorm room, he was expecting to meet a new roommate since the fall semester had already started and his old roommate, Paul, had graduated the previous spring.

Opening the door, he received two surprises: there was no roommate in the room, and both beds were filled with cards and letters from people all over the world congratulating him.

He opened a few and read them. *It will take months to read all of these*, he thought. And how could he answer all of them? It would cost a fortune to mail answers to everyone.

He was hungry, but he decided to try to arrange the letters and cards in some form of order before he went and ate. There were some letters that were written on business-type envelopes, and others didn't even have stamps on them; they were from students at the university who had just written a note and put it in his campus mailbox. After an hour, he decided to stop and go eat.

As he was leaving his dorm, he remembered he wasn't a student this semester, and he didn't have a new meal card. He wasn't sure what he was going to do. He tried calling Coach Sines, but he didn't answer. He then called Coach Turner and told him his problem. The coach told him to tell the cashier he would be by tomorrow and pay for Boots's meal.

Boots didn't particularly like that idea; here he was an Olympic champion having to beg for someone to pay for his meal.

The coaches had not even thought about his meals. Boots was also wondering where he was going to live. He was no longer a student, so he could not live in the dorm forever. He was also going to have to find a job now that his running days were over. He was in deep thought as he walked into the cafeteria.

His deep thoughts changed as he walked through the cafeteria doors. Students from all over the cafeteria stood up and cheered and clapped.

He smiled and waved. He still had his gold medal around his neck under his coat. He pulled it out and held it up to another big round of cheers. "Go, Vols!" he said.

The students in the cafeteria started chanting "Go, Vols! Go, Vols!" This continued for several minutes.

Students from all over the cafeteria gathered around Boots to see what an Olympic gold medal looked like. The students were talking and asking him things just like he was an old friend. Boots knew none of them.

Boots kept trying to work his way through all the students to tell the cashier what the coach had said about paying for the meal. This was going to be embarrassing in front of all those students.

As he neared the cashier, one of the male students said, "Here, I got this. You get whatever you want and come and sit at our table." The boy paid for Boots's meal.

Boots had planned on just eating and going back and reading some of the letters, but since the boy was nice enough to pay for his meal, he felt like he was obligated to sit and talk with the guys for a while.

An hour later, when he could finally get away from all his fans, he realized his life was never going to be the same. Even on the way back to the dorm, students were stopping and wanting to talk. He finally pulled his hood over his head and walked the rest of the way back to the dorm with his head down.

Boots decided to open some of the letters that had been sent with business addresses on them. He couldn't believe it; he had been offered jobs, places to live, and all kinds of guest appearances on local and national TV shows. People would pay him to come and appear on different shows and do all kinds of speaking engagements.

He was getting tired, so he moved some of the mail to the floor so he could have a place to sleep. In bed, he thought about all the offers he had read already, and he had barely scanned the stack of letters. He also remembered about Coach Turner's warning about leeches, but these people seemed so kind and sincere.

Boots didn't know if he even had five dollars in his wallet, and now he could be rich. Just go and tell people what it was like being an Olympic champion. He had trouble sleeping all night.

The following morning, he read a few more letters and then went over to Coach Sines's office to talk to him about all these business offers.

He walked into the office and asked the secretary if Coach Sines was in. She told him no, that he was away on a recruiting trip.

As Boots walked out of the office, he thought that was strange. He just got home from Europe. Why wouldn't he take some time off? He then remembered that he had been gone most of the summer and fall, helping him at the NCAA and Olympic meets, so he hadn't been able to recruit yet. He had even turned the cross-country team over to one of the assistant baseball coaches who had offered to help while he was away in Rome.

He was walking back to his dorm room to call Coach Turner when he heard someone yell to him. *Probably another fan*, he thought.

It was Coach Turner. He had gotten him a new meal ticket.

"Thanks. I think I'll go use it now. I'm hungry. Coach, have you got a few minutes to talk? I need some advice," Boots said.

"Sure. I need to go over to the cafeteria and pay for your meal last night. Sorry about that. We just forgot you didn't have a new meal ticket," Coach said.

Boots told him about what happened last night in the cafeteria.

"I'm afraid it's going to be that way for a long time, but it beats coming back and no one wants to talk to you because you lost," the coach said with a smile.

"About all these job offers and business deals, you need to be careful and not jump into things. Like I keep telling you, some of the people will use you for their benefit. They act like you're their hero, but they want to make money off of you."

"I know, Coach, but I don't have five dollars to my name. I can't stay in this dorm because I'm not in school. I have to get a job somewhere. Mr. Longhurst told me I could come back and be a foreman at the plantation like I did the summer before last, but I don't want that life anymore."

"How many classes do you lack to get your degree?"

"Two, I think," Boots answered.

"You need to get your degree, no matter what else you do. Let me talk to Coach Sines when he gets back, and maybe we can find a way you can stay in school and get the credits you need to graduate."

Coach Turner talked to Coach Sines when he got back from recruiting.

Coach Sines said, "We can't put him on as a graduate assistant because he hasn't graduated yet. He really is not supposed to be living in the dorm right now since he is not a student. Let me think about it and see what I can do."

"The semester has been going on over a month now, or I would pay for his tuition, and he could live with me until he finishes. But we were so late getting back from Rome; no professor would allow him to start classes this late," Coach Turner said.

B oots began to accept a few offers that paid him money to speak or be interviewed on national TV shows. He had never really had any money of his own, except the summer he worked on the plantation, and then the deaths of his parents that same year had wiped out all his savings.

One of the big businessmen who supported UT let Boots stay in one of his apartments rent-free until he could get back in school and finish his schooling.

Boots was making enough money doing odd jobs and speaking appearances to be able to afford to eat regularly, but he needed something else.

Now that he was no longer at the university every day, he didn't see much of his former coaches. They were preparing for the upcoming track season.

Boots had no phone, so it was hard for people to get in contact with him. His address had changed, and a lot of the people who had mailed him things when he got back no longer had his correct address.

Boots still had no car or driver's licenses, so he had to bum rides or take the city bus wherever he went.

He opened a letter one day from a Mr. McCoy. He owned a car dealership in Knoxville. Boots had seen some of his commercials on TV. He was always wearing some kind of corny get-up trying to sell his used cars.

Mr. McCoy was offering Boots a job. He enclosed a phone number and asked him to give him a call at his earliest convince.

Boots decided to call and see what the job was.

Mr. McCoy told him he would like for him to appear in his commercials, with him wearing his Olympic gold medal and doing different skits. He wanted him to invite people to come to the car lot and have their picture taken with an Olympic champion, and he would be glad to autograph the picture.

"That's all I would have to do?" Boots asked.

"That and I'll make you a car salesman too. While the people are there, you can ask if they are interested in buying one of our cars and show them around the lot. I'll pay you a small weekly salary in the beginning, and you can also work on commission as well."

Boots had no clue what work on commission meant, but he didn't say anything.

"Well, sir, that sounds pretty good, but I had planned on going back to school this winter and finishing the two courses I lack to get my degree."

He didn't know where he was going to come up with the money to pay for his tuition. He was just barely making ends meet now.

"Why, that's no problem. Car sales go down in the winter anyway. You can come and go as you please. You go to classes and then come and sell cars and do commercials with me. You can even wear a shirt to classes with my car lot's name on it. It would be good advertisement, and you can talk some of your friends at school into buying one of our cars." He laughed.

"I'll keep your face on TV so people will see you so much they will think they know you personally when they run into you on the street.

With this deal, you and I both win. What do you say? Do we have a deal?"

"But I don't know anything about cars or selling," Boots said. He didn't tell McCoy he didn't have a driver's license or had never driven a car before.

"What's to know? You just tell them what a great car it is and what a good deal you are offering them. We have the prices marked up high on the cars so our salesman can knock a few bucks off of the sticker price, and the buyers think they're getting a good deal."

Boots still wasn't sure what he should do.

"How about this. You come down to the lot and look around. We film a commercial and put it on radio and TV, and you decide if you like it," McCoy said.

Boots thought it sounded like a good idea, so he agreed.

He asked where the car lot was, and they agreed to meet the following Monday.

Boots told him he would take the bus and meet him there.

"What? You don't own a car?" McCoy smiled. "We'll get you fixed up in a nice car too. Give me your address, and I'll have someone pick you up Monday morning about ten o'clock."

On Monday morning, a car pulled up in front of Boots's apartment. The man rolled down the window and asked if he was Boots.

Boots nodded his head yes and got into the car.

The driver introduced himself as Larry, a salesman for Mr. McCoy. He drove him to the car lot and asked Boots if he was married and if he had any kids.

Upon arriving, Boots was taken to Mr. McCoy's office.

The man behind the desk was on the phone and didn't sound too happy.

He finally hung the phone up and said, "I wish the police would mind their own business. Should have better things to do than harass a teenage kid.

"Hi, I'm Mr. McCoy, and I assume you are Boots?" He reached out and shook Boots's hand.

"I'm sorry, but I have to go to the police station and straighten out some stupid policeman about harassing my son. Maybe we can meet tomorrow.

"Here, let me give you bus fare back home," Mr. McCoy said. He reached into his pocket and pulled out the largest roll of money Boots had ever seen. "Here. This should cover the bus ride."

He started to hand Boots a fifty-dollar bill but pulled it back and said, "Hell with the bus. Here's a hundred. Take a cab."

Boots didn't recognize it, but this was going to be the first major leech he would encounter.

"Don't forget to bring your gold medal with you for the commercial tomorrow." McCoy chuckled. "Hey, Larry, give Mr. Boots here a ride back to wherever he lives."

Boots didn't know if Mr. McCoy knew he had just given him money for a cab or if he was doing it on purpose to give him some money, or maybe just to show off his money.

On the ride back to his apartment, Larry carried on some small talk and told Boots he looked familiar.

"Have I seen you somewhere before?" Larry asked.

Boots told him it was possible he had seen him on TV. He went on to tell him he was an Olympic champion.

"Oh, that's where I've seen you, on TV," Larry said excitedly. "Hey, you live on Baxter Street, right?"

"Yes," Boots replied.

"Hey, man, I don't live too far from there. Do you mind if we swing by my house and let my wife take a picture of you and me?"

Boots was flattered. "Sure, we can do that," said Boots.

"Mr. McCoy will never know. It will be all right. It's a shame you don't have that gold medal with you. Can we swing by and get it for the picture?"

Boots pulled the medal out of his pocket and said, "That won't be necessary. I have it with me. I am afraid to leave it in my home because someone might try to steal it; it is made of gold."

Boots wanted to talk to Coach Turner, but he knew they were away at the indoor SEC track meet this week, so he would have to decide about the job offer for himself.

The following day as he walked out the door to go catch the bus to go to the car lot, he saw Larry get out of a car and wave him over. Mr. McCoy had sent Larry to pick him up so he wouldn't have to get a bus or cab.

Boots thought that was awfully nice of Mr. McCoy, but he hoped this didn't mean he wanted his hundred-dollar bill back.

When they arrived at the car lot, Mr. McCoy greeted Boots and ushered into his office. He went over how the commercial would go and asked if he had his medal with him.

Boots took the medal out of his pocket. He kept it wrapped in a handkerchief.

"Wow. Can I hold it?" Mr. McCoy asked.

He put it around his neck and asked how he looked.

Boots just gave him a thumbs-up. He didn't particularly like that he had put it around his neck. Boots's neck had been the only one it had ever been around.

Mr. McCoy handed Boots a shirt with "McCoy's Auto Sales," on it. He was told to put it on and then put the Olympic medal on.

"Let me do all the talking, except when I introduce you. Tell me how glad you are to be working with me," McCoy said.

Since winning the Olympics, Boots had been in front of a lot of TV cameras, so he didn't feel that nervous.

They walked out and stood in front of one of the cars for sale on the lot to do the filming. It was winter, and the temperature was in the low forties, and Boots was standing there in a short-sleeved shirt, while Mr. McCoy had a coat and tie on.

After about fifteen minutes, the filming began.

Mr. McCoy started off by saying they were glad to welcome a new salesman to their staff.

Boots had not agreed to take the job. All he had agreed to do was the commercial.

Mr. McCoy went on to brag about Boots being an Olympic champion and how good it was to have a world champion working at his car lot.

He then said, "Boots, I want to welcome you on becoming the newest member of our staff at McCoy's Auto Sales." He paused for Boots to say something.

Boot looked at McCoy and said, "Thank you very much for having me."

"Now, here's what we are going to do, folks. If you drive in to McCoy's Auto Sales, you can have your picture taken with our Olympic champion on our staff now, and he will be glad to sign autographs too, folks. But wait. That's not all, folks. If you mention that you saw this add on TV, we will knock an addition hundred dollars off our already low prices on our automobiles. Don't forget the chance to meet a world champion and get a world-champion deal on our fine used cars too. You can't beat that combination, folks. Give McCoy's a try today."

After, McCoy said, "That went well. Let's go in and talk."

Boots was so cold his teeth were chattering.

"So, here is the deal. You will be paid a salary of a hundred dollars a week plus a 10 percent commission on any car you sell. Sounds like a good deal to me. With you being an Olympic champion and as popular as you are, you should sell all kinds of cars," Mr. McCoy said.

"What about me finishing school?" Boots asked.

"No problem. Like I told you over the phone, when you have a class, you are excused to leave anytime. Have we got a deal?" McCoy asked.

Boots could sure use the hundred dollars a week, and maybe working at a car lot he could learn how to drive. He agreed.

"That's great. Glad to have you on board. Let's go out to lunch and celebrate."

They walked into a fancy restaurant that Boots had never heard of before.

As they sat down at the table, Mr. McCoy told Boots to take his coat off and put the medal back on so people could see the medal along with the McCoy's auto writing on the shirt.

"Advertisement, son—advertisement," McCoy said with a grin.

Boots could tell this was a high-class restaurant by the way people were dressed.

Several businessmen walked by and looked at the medal hanging around Boots's neck and slowed down.

Mr. McCoy stood up and invited them to meet the Olympic champion of the 100 meters.

Boots had to correct him and say it was the 1500 meters.

McCoy said, "Whatever, you're still the champion."

McCoy dropped Boots off at his apartment and told him to be at work promptly at eight o'clock in the morning.

Boots got to thinking after he got home about how much it was going to cost to ride the bus every day, and the food he would have to buy for lunch, and he hadn't even been told how many days a week he would work or what the hours were. He started to think maybe he had made the wrong decision.

The booster who owned the apartment complex had agreed to let Boots stay there rent-free until he had a job. He now would have to pay rent. He didn't know how much rent would be and the food he would need, but he knew it would take more than the $400 he would make a month working at the car lot. He was going to have to sell a lot of cars just to break even.

He was at the bus stop at six thirty because he didn't know how long it would take to ride the bus to the car lot. Plus, he didn't want to be late on his first day.

He arrived at the lot around seven thirty, so that meant he would have to catch the bus every morning around six thirty.

Getting up early for classes and workouts seemed normal, but he couldn't figure out why he had to be there so early. Who would be car shopping at eight in the morning?

He walked into the office and saw that Mr. McCoy's door was closed. He saw a lady coming from the back room carrying a coffee cup. The lady asks Boots if she could help him.

"I'm supposed to be here at eight to meet Mr. McCoy," Boots said.

The lady chuckled and said, "Yeah, right. He doesn't get her until ten or eleven each day."

"I'm supposed to start working here today," Boots said.

"Honey, I know nothing about you working here."

She got on an intercom and paged a guy named Clarence.

A guy walked in and said, "What do you want? I'm eating breakfast."

"Sorry to spoil your day," she snapped back. "This kid here says he supposed to start work here today. You know anything about it?"

"Oh, you must be the runner guy," Clarence said.

"Yes, sir. My name is Boots."

"Follow me," he said. "Can't even eat breakfast in peace around here," he grunted as he stormed out.

Boots stood in the garage office, while Clarence and several other guys ate breakfast and complained about everything.

Finally, Clarence threw the paper bag and napkins in the trash and said, "Guys, this is our new salesman, the boy wonder track star. What was it you won?" Clarence asked.

"The 1500-meter run at the Olympics, sir."

"Hey, I saw you run then. I was watching on TV. You're the one who runs for Tennessee, aren't you?" the man asked.

"I used to run for them, but now my running days are over," replied Boots.

"My name is Andrew," the young man said. "The guy in the corner is George, and the old guy is Ron."

Boots started to reach out his hand, but none of the men moved a muscle. Ron did nod his head.

"So, what did Mr. McCoy tell you that you would be doing around here?" Clarence asked.

"I'm supposed to be a car salesman. We made a TV commercial the other day, and Mr. McCoy invited people to come in and have their pictures made with me and sign autographs."

"Oh, a celebrity." George laughed.

"Know anything about selling cars?" Clarence asked.

"No, sir, I don't," replied Boots.

"The first thing you need to know about selling cars is never tell the truth." George laughed.

Boots laughed; he thought he was kidding. He wasn't.

"It doesn't make any difference what is wrong with the car or what a piece of junk it is, you always tell the customer what a great-running car it is and what a steal it is at that price," George said.

After looking at the other guys' expressions, he realized that George was telling the truth.

"So I just lie to people?" Boots asked.

"We don't like to call it lying," Clarence said. "Just stretching the truth a little." He laughed.

Just then, in walked Mr. McCoy. Boots could see everyone straighten up and act completely different from before.

"Good morning, Mr. McCoy. What brings you in so early?" Clarence asked.

"Our new salesman here. Our Olympic drawing card. We caught any fish in out trap yet?" he asked.

"Sir?" Clarence questioned.

"Have we gotten any suckers in here yet to get the free picture and autograph so we can sucker them into buying a car?" McCoy replied.

"No, sir," Clarence replied.

Boots didn't like what he had just heard; he felt like he was being used, which he was.

"Well, it's early yet, and it's cold outside right now. The radio commercial starts this morning, and I think the TV starts in a couple more days. We will have fish in here before the day is out. Get that boy over there a shirt with our logo on it," McCoy said as he stomped out, heading to his office.

As the day wore on, several people stopped by to have their pictures taken with Boots, and each time, McCoy would run out and put his arm around Boots like they were father and son.

"While you nice folks are here, let Boots here show you some cars while he tells you about what it was like running in the Olympics. And remember our hundred-dollar discount going on right now," McCoy would say.

Boots would show people different cars, but he didn't know anything about them. He didn't know a Ford from a Chevy. He would read things off of the sticker on the window about all the features the car had, but he had no clue what anything meant.

It was six o'clock, and Boots was still there. Clarence had gone home along with the other salesmen he had met that morning. Wilbur had replaced Clarence as the night manager, so Boots went and asked him what time he could leave.

"Mr. McCoy wanted you to stay as late as possible so people could take advantage of the pictures and autographs."

"But I have been here since eight this morning," Boots said.

"Just stay one more hour. We close at eight," Wilbur said.

When Boots got home, it was after nine. He knew he had made a big mistake. He had not eaten since lunchtime when George went out and got sandwiches.

The following day, it was past eleven before he saw Mr. McCoy pull in. He wanted to talk to him, but Mr. McCoy went straight to his office.

Later, when some autograph seekers came by, Mr. McCoy came running out and put his arm around Boots and began thanking the people for coming by.

Mr. McCoy told the people that after the pictures with Boots, Boots would be happy to show them some cars, but they declined.

Here was his chance. Boots said, "Mr. McCoy, I can't work twelve hours a day. This is worse than training for the Olympics."

Mr. McCoy assured him the long hours would just be for this week to take advantage of the TV and radio commercials.

"Do I have to work on Saturday too?" Boots asked.

"Sure, son. That's our big day on the car lot. We'll have lots of people here for pictures and autographs. Most people who work can't get here through the week. How many cars have you sold this week?" he asked.

"None, sir," Boots replied.

"Need to pick it up, son," McCoy said. "Oh Saturday night, you need to attend a party with me. There will be lots of important people there, and I need to show off my latest salesman. Wear a coat and tie. Bring your medal with you."

"I don't have a coat and tie, sir," Boots replied.

"You can't borrow one from somebody?" McCoy asked.

"No, sir. I don't know anyone who has one I could borrow."

"I'll ask the men tomorrow if someone has one you can borrow."

The next two days were basically the same. Boots worked almost twelve hours both days.

The following morning, Boots came in at ten o'clock; he had overslept. He was so tired he could hardly drag himself to work.

When he arrived, he walked into one of the offices where the salesmen hung out, unless they had a customer or saw someone in the car lot that might be a potential buyer. The only one in there was Larry.

Of all the people at the car lot, Larry had been the friendliest of the salesmen. They had actually talked quite a bit to each other about their lives, and Larry was especially interested in Boots's Olympic experience.

Larry was the only one at the lot who asked to have his picture taken with Boots and had him autograph it.

"Did anyone say anything about me being late?" Boots asked.

"No, you're fine. Old man McCoy usually doesn't get her until around lunch time every day. I know they have been working you to death. Don't worry about it, man," Larry said. "Maybe if they ever let you work decent hours, we can go out and have a beer or two one night."

"Sounds great," Boots said.

Boots had only drunk beer a few times. He remembered the first time he drank beer he drank way too many had a terrible hangover the following day. The second time, he had learned his lesson and drank only a few. With all that had gone on this week, he could sure use a beer.

Since he had moved away from the university, he hardly ever saw any of his friends, and since he had started work, he had not been in contact with anyone except the men at work. He could use a night out. He had not even talked to the coaches in over a month. He had no car or phone, so he was just stuck where he lived.

The picture and autograph stunt that Mr. McCoy had come up with had worked the first few days, but now hardly anyone stopped by. It was winter and nearing Christmas, so people had other things to do.

The ironic thing that happened that day was Boots sold his first car, and it had nothing to do with him being a famous athlete.

A father brought his teenage son in and bought him a car for Christmas. Boots followed the sales pitch he had been taught. He bragged on what a great car it was and how he could lower the price and it would be a great first car for his son.

The father told Boots he looked awful familiar and ask if they had met before, but Boots just said he didn't think so.

Boots was about to experience a big first. Once a salesman sold a car, it had to be driven around to the body shop to receive a final cleaning and wash. Boots had never driven a car.

He took the father and son into the office for the paperwork to be completed. He was supposed to drive the car around back to the garage where they would wash and clean it while the paperwork was being done in the office. He knew if he asked someone to drive it for him, they would want to know why. Since all the salesmen were inside, he decided to try it himself. *It would be embarrassing to wreck a car in the parking lot*, Boots thought.

Boots got behind the wheel, and to his relief, the car was not one of those cars with a stick shift. There would be no way he could drive one of those.

He had watched people drive the times he had been in someone else's car, so he knew where to put the key, and he knew the big pedal in the floor was the brake. *So far, so good*, he thought.

He turned the ignition key and stepped on the gas. He pushed the gas pedal down too far, and the engine revved up loudly. He looked around to see if anyone had heard.

He eased the car into gear, took his foot of the brake, and barely touched the gas. The car began to move forward. When he had cleared the cars on either side, he began turning the wheel. He had one foot on the brake and the other giving it gas. He crept along until he needed to turn toward the back garage.

When he reached the garage, the huge doors were closed, so he just turned the engine off and walked into the garage. He handed the keys to one of the cleanup men and turned to walk out.

"Why didn't you open the door and pull it in yourself? I have to do everything around here because of these lazy salesmen," the man complained.

Boots thought that driving wasn't so bad, but he didn't want to try to squeeze that car through the tiny opening into the garage.

Later that afternoon, Mr. McCoy stopped by and talked to Boots.

"We've got that party tomorrow night, and there will be a lot of important people there, so act nice and make me look good. I borrowed you a sport coat and tie; they're hanging in my office. Bring a nice pair of dress pants to work tomorrow, and we will leave from here. Oh, and bring your medal with you so I can show you off. I heard you sold your first car today. About time," he said as he walked back toward his office.

Boots thought, *We will leave from work because I will still be working all day and half the night.*

The following day, Boots arrived at work with his only pair of dress pants and a shirt. He would be glad when this day was over. The car lot was closed on Sunday, so this would be his only day of rest for the week.

The men were paid on Saturday, so he was looking forward to seeing how much commission he had made for the sale of the car. When he looked at the check, he thought something was wrong. The car he had sold cost $2,000, and he was supposed to get a 10 percent commission, yet he had received only a 5 percent commission.

When he went in to ask the accountant, he was told that Mr. McCoy had only authorized a 5 percent commission for him.

He decided to talk to Mr. McCoy on the way to the party later.

He had not seen Mr. McCoy at the car lot all day. He saw the coat and tie hanging in his office.

About an hour later, Larry walked up to Boots and said, "We will be leaving in about an hour. Maybe you should go get dressed."

"Oh, are you going too?" Boots asked.

"No. I'm just driving you there and taking you home later."

"I thought I would be riding with Mr. McCoy from the way he talked."

While on their way to the party, Boots told Larry about only receiving a 5 percent commission, while he had been promised 10 percent.

Larry said, "Between me and you, you can't trust a thing he says. He did the same thing to me when I first started working here. I called him on it, and he blamed it on the accountant. I went and talked to her, and she said he had told her directly to only give me 5 percent.

"You do have your medal with you, don't you?" Larry asked.

"Sure," Boots replied.

"Good. McCoy told me to make sure you had it with you for the party, and if you didn't, we were to drive back to your place and pick it up."

Boots got out of the car and walked up the steps to a very expensive-looking house.

When he got to the door, a servant dressed in a black suit asked for his invitation.

As Boots was about to explain that he had been invited by Mr. McCoy, a couple walked up and handed the man an envelope. He welcomed them and opened the door for them to enter.

Boots said, "I'm supposed to be the guest of Mr. McCoy."

"Just a minute, and I'll go check," the servant said.

In a few minutes, he came back and said, "You may go in, sir. Sorry for the inconvenience, sir."

"It's not your fault," Boots said. In his mind, he thought, *No, it's my dear boss's fault.*

As he walked in, Mr. McCoy came rushing up to him, put his arm around him, and said, "Put your medal on. We want everyone to see it."

Boots felt uncomfortable because it felt like he was just showing off.

Mr. McCoy walked around to all the big influential people and introduced him as an Olympic champion and his new leading salesman. Boots had sold one car so far.

Everyone wanted a picture with Boots and an autograph. They all wanted to closely look at his medal and touch it.

Servants were walking around handing out drinks. He had seen Mr. McCoy already drink three since he had been there, and he was reaching for the fourth.

Boots was offered a drink but politely said no.

Mr. McCoy took a drink off of the tray, handed it to Boots, and said, "Drink up, son. You have to be sociable to the guests. Your training days are over. Have a little fun. These people can help my business grow. Walk around and mingle with the guests."

Mr. McCoy walked over to talk to some ladies standing nearby. Boots assumed one was his wife, but he had not even bothered to introduce his wife to him.

Boots had hoped that they would have food to eat at this party; he hadn't eaten since a sandwich at lunch. All he saw were some plates on a large table with little bitty, weird-looking food. He noticed people were picking up small plates and putting this little food on it. He moved near the table and loaded the little plate full.

As he was finishing the food, he wondered if they could get seconds; he was still hungry. He thought about throwing the paper plate in the trash can and going through just like this was his first time.

A couple of men walked up to him and began asking about the Olympics. As the men turned to walk away, one man handed Boots his business card and said, "If you ever decide to get out of car sales, give me a call, and I can put you to work."

Before the night was over, Boots had collected quite a few business cards from different people.

Since Mr. McCoy had no use for him anymore, he decided to leave. He knew Larry was waiting outside in the car for him. He decided to fill one more plate up and take it to Larry.

When he got to the car, he saw Larry in the front seat asleep. He pecked on the window and woke him up.

"Let's blow this place," Boots said.

He described the boring evening to Larry. "All he wanted me for was to show me off and make himself look important," Boots said.

"He's full of himself, that's for sure. Do you want to stop and have a beer on the way home?" Larry asked.

"That sounds good," Boots replied.

Larry drove to one of his favorite bars. They walked in and sat down.

When the waitress came to take their orders, Larry said, "I'll have a tall Bud."

Since Boots didn't know one beer from another, he ordered the same thing.

One beer was followed by several.

Boots was feeling a little weird. He had only been drunk once in his life, and he didn't want to feel like that again.

As Larry was telling one of his stories, two of Larry's friends walked up and sat down at the table.

Larry introduced Skip and Bruce to Boots.

They each ordered another round of drinks, and Skip asked Boots how he got the name Boots.

"It's a long story," Boots said.

"He's the fastest miler in the world," Larry said with a drunken slur. "He won those Swedish games."

"What?" Bruce asked.

"You know those games in that other country over there," Larry said.

They both looked at Boots for an explanation.

"I'm not the fastest miler in the world, but I do have one of the fastest 1500-meter times in the world. The Swedish games he was talking about were the Olympics."

"You won the Olympics?" Bruce asked.

Boots nodded his head yes.

"I watched you on television then," Skip said. "I watched the Olympics every night."

"He's got that gold medal in his pocket right now," Larry said.

"Can we see it?" Skip asked.

Boots really didn't want to take it out in the bar; he might get mugged on the way out. The gold in it was worth a lot of money.

He took it out anyway and let the boys see it.

Larry was pretty hammered by now, and Boots didn't want to ride home with him driving. Luckily, the bar was only a few blocks from home, so when Larry went to the bathroom, he told the guys to tell Larry he would just walk home.

He paid his tab and started the walk home.

It was cool outside, and the weathermen were predicting heavy snow later in the week.

When Boots reached his apartment, he saw a note attached to the door. He pulled the note off and walked inside. He had only walked a few blocks, but he was frozen.

He opened the note and saw it was from Coach Turner. He said he had been by several times but could not catch him home; he wondered if Boots had a job or had moved. He told him to stop by the coaches' office when he could; they had some news for him. At the end of the note was a p.s.—"You're spending Christmas dinner with us."

Boots was glad that the following day was Sunday and he could sleep as late as he wanted. He was also glad the party was over. He was being used, and he knew it. He pulled the business cards out of his pocket and laid them on the chair; he might just need to give some of these men a call.

Boots drifted off to sleep. The next morning, he wasn't sure if it was the alcohol or working twelve hours a day that made him sleep so well, but he couldn't remember sleeping so well.

Boots had no television or radio, so he didn't know that the weatherman had moved the incoming snow storm up a few days. When Boots got up Monday, ready for work, he didn't know there were five inches of snow on the ground until he walked outside.

He had never been told at work what to do if there was a big snow storm, but he couldn't see how they would keep the car lot open on days like this, so he went back inside and went back to bed.

When he finally got up two hours later, he wasn't sure what to do the rest of the day. If the buses were running, this would be a good day to go visit the coaches at the university.

He decided to walk to the bus stop and see if the buses were running.

Pretty soon, he saw a bus in the distance heading toward the bus stop. He climbed on board and headed to the university. He wondered if anyone would remember him besides the coaches. Not too long ago, he was the big hero at UT, but people forget quickly.

On the bus ride over, he thought about his salary. He would probably not get paid for days he wasn't at the car lot. He didn't make much as it was. How could he pay his bills?

The bus pulled up to the bus stop at the university. As he was exiting the bus, several students who were boarding the bus said hello and called him by name. Maybe he hadn't been forgotten.

As he neared the athletic facilities that contained the coaches' offices, he hoped Coaches Sines and Turner would be in. He could see a light on in Coach Sines's office, but Coach Turner's was not near a window, so he didn't know if he was in or not.

He reached Coach Turner's office first and walked in.

Coach jumped up, ran over, and gave Boots a big hug.

"Where have you been hiding?" he asked.

They sat down and talked for a few minutes, and Boots told him he had a job at a car lot.

"Which car lot do you work at?" Coach asked.

When Boots told him he worked at McCoy's Auto Sales, the coach's expression changed.

"Is there something wrong?" Boots asked.

Coach Turner didn't even answer. He said, "Let's go to Coach Sines's office. He has some news for you."

As they walked in, Coach Sines jumped up and walked over and hugged Boots. He said, "Where have you been? We have been trying to get hold of you for weeks."

Coach Turner said, "Boots has a job; he is working for McCoy Auto Sales."

Coach Sines immediately said, "He's nothing but a crook. Why are you working for that guy?"

"I needed money, and he was the only one to offer me a job," Boots replied.

"You mean, of all the people who wanted to give you a job, you chose him?" Coach Sines answered.

"He's the only one I talked to that offered me a job," Boots said.

"Didn't you get calls from people who wanted to help you with a job?" Coach Sines asked.

"I don't have a phone," Boots said.

"Surely you received letters from important businessmen offering you a job."

"The only letters I received were on my bed when I got back from Rome. I had to move out of the dorm the next week, and no one had my new address."

The coaches looked at each other and realized part of this was their fault. They just assumed he would get all kinds of calls with different job offers, and he could choose the one he wanted.

"So, when was the last time you had anyone who seemed interested in giving you a job?" Coach Turner asked.

Boots had the business cards from the party Saturday night in his pocket. He had planned on calling some of the numbers today since he would be near some pay phones.

He pulled the cards out of his pocket and explained that he had been given the cards at a party on Saturday night. He handed the cards to Coach Sines.

The coach looked at them one by one. He threw the first card down on his desk to the right and said, "Crook." He looked at the next one and said, "Crook." He looked at the third one and said, "Dirty." He looked at the fourth one and said, "Good man." When he had gotten through all the cards, he only had two cards in the good man category, and the rest were in the crook pile. He picked up the crook pile and threw them in the garbage can.

"I know these two men, and I will talk to them tomorrow and get back with you," Coach Sines said.

"Are you enrolled in the winter semester to finish your last two classes?" Coach Turner asked.

"I'm going by the administration office when I leave here to get my paperwork to enroll," Boots replied.

"Good. You have come too far not to get your degree," Turner said.

Boots started to leave, but Coach Turner stopped him. "We almost forgot why you're here," he said. He looked at Coach Sines and said, "You do the honors."

"Boots, you have been voted by the New York Athletic Association as the winner of the Most Outstanding Track-and-Field Runner in the US for the year 1960. Congratulations, son. You deserve it."

Boots didn't know what to say; he was speechless.

"You will be flown to New York and be presented the award at a huge banquet. It will be televised by one of the major TV networks and sent all over the world."

Boots was stunned. He thought his athletic career and awards were over.

Coach Sines said, "You deserve this award and are the first athlete from the University of Tennessee to receive it."

Coach Turner walked over and hugged Boots and told him how proud he was of him.

Boots walked out of the office and headed to the administration building to pick up his papers for the winter semester. Even though it was cold outside with all of the snow, Boots felt warm inside.

Since the snow was several inches, Boots didn't know if he should go to work or not. He tried calling, but no one answered the phone.

He decided to go in the next morning because he needed a paycheck to help pay his tuition for the winter quarter. He didn't know how he would be able to afford both school and food. He would no longer have the meal card he had when he was an athlete.

He arrived at the lot the next morning, and only Clarence was there. He told Boots to start cleaning the snow off the cars.

After about two hours, Boots saw Mr. McCoy pull up and go into his office. He gave him about thirty minutes and then headed to his office to talk to him.

The door was open. Mr. McCoy was on the phone but motioned him in. He talked for a few more minutes and then hung up.

"Hey, Boots, what can I do for you today?"

Boots decided to tell him about the award and that he would need to be off a couple of days to fly to New York for the award.

"That's great. Congratulations. We can make a new commercial with you holding your award with the goal medal around your neck," Mr. McCoy said. "We need to get you a blazer with McCoy Auto Sales embroidered on it to wear when you accept the award. I'll get my secretary on that."

Boots wasn't about to wear a blazer like that to receive his award.

Boots told him there was one other thing he needed to discuss before he left. He told him he would be going to school during the winter quarter to complete the two courses he needed to get his degree.

Mr. McCoy said, "No way. I need you here."

"But you said I could attend classes to finish my degree."

"Things have changed. Larry quit yesterday, and I need you because I will only have three other salesmen to work our two shifts here."

Boots looked at him and took his coat off. He pulled the shirt off that had McCoy Auto Sales on it, dropped it in the floor, and put his coat back on. He turned to walk out the door and said, "You sell you pieces of junk. I quit."

Boots headed to the bus stop and caught the next bus home. He had no clue what he was going to do now. He had no job, no income, and no money to attend the winter semester.

He had only thirty dollars left, but he decided to stop off at local bar and drink beer until it ran out. The only food he had left in his refrigerator at home was a pack of baloney and a half loaf of bread. He thought he could make a sign and sit at a busy intersection and beg like the rest. A few months ago, he won the Olympics, and now he had no money or job.

When he walked in the bar, he saw Larry, Bruce, and Skip sitting at a table. When Larry saw him, he motioned him over.

"What are you doing here so early? Shouldn't you still be working for another ten hours?" Larry laughed.

He told the guys what had happened. "He promised me when he hired me that I could go back to school and finish my degree," Boots said.

Larry told him that he had quit too because he was nothing but a crook and didn't care about anyone but himself. Employees were treated like second-class humans.

"So, what are you going to do?" Skip asked.

"Probably make a sign and sit on a street corner," Boots said.

The guys started to laugh, but they realized he was serious.

How could a world champion be sitting on a corner, begging, less than five months after being on top of the athletic world?

Boots got up to leave, but they told him to have one more before he left. He told them he only had thirty dollars and his bill was probably nearing that now, so he couldn't afford another one.

Skip told him the next round was on him, so Boots stayed for another beer.

After three days of eating baloney sandwiches, Boots knew he had to do something.

He made a sign that read "Will work for food. God bless."

He remembered all the times he had said he would bring God into his life as soon as this race or that problem was over; he never followed through though.

He thought about heading downtown to a busy intersection to sit on the corner, but he didn't even have money for the bus fare now.

After sitting with his sign all day, he had made five dollars and twenty-six cents. Looked like another baloney supper.

Boots decided to take part of the money and ride the bus to a busier part of town in hopes of making more money. He made fifteen dollars and change; his business was picking up. He decided to head to the same corner the next day.

The following day, it was windy and cold, so Boots wore all the clothes he had to stay warm. He collected four times what he had collected the day before. He had no clue why until someone dropped money into his hat and said, "Merry Christmas."

Boots realized it was Christmas Eve. He had been invited to Coach Turner's house for Christmas dinner the next day. He knew he couldn't let Coach see him like this.

When he got home, there was a note on the door. He opened it and read: "Missed you again. Be by at ten to pick you up for Christmas dinner. Merry Christmas, Coach Turner."

There was no way he could let the coach see him in this condition. He hadn't shaved in weeks. The only time he was able to wash up was at the local fast-food bathroom. He needed to not be home tomorrow or not answer the door.

Boots decided to leave and not be home when Coach showed up. He had passed a sign while walking home that said the local homeless shelter down the street would be serving Christmas dinner to the homeless. He wasn't really homeless, but he might as well be. He decided to go there.

He got up the following morning and headed out of his apartment. He didn't know what time it was, but he knew it was very cold outside.

Boots wasn't sure what time they would begin serving, but he knew it probably would not be for at least a couple of hours.

He decided to sit in one of the bus stop shelters to protect him from the wind. He thought back to a year ago at this time when he was at Coach Turner's, eating dinner with his family, and all the training he had been doing, hoping to make the Olympic team.

Now here he was a year later, an Olympic champion sitting at a bus stop, trying to stay warm, waiting for a free meal at a homeless shelter.

Boots wasn't sure if he would be asked if he was homeless when he went through the door to get his free meal, but he had decided if they asked him, he would tell them he was homeless. He might as well be. There was nothing in his home but a bed and an empty refrigerator. His power and heat had been turned off for not paying his electric bill.

Once Boots sat down and began to eat, he never remembered food tasting so good. He noticed there was very little talking between the people who were eating; they were so happy to get a good meal they just wanted to savor the moment. It took their minds off their problems for a brief time.

Boots had thought about seeing if he could get into a homeless shelter. He had received several letters from the booster who was letting him live there rent-free, but he had not opened them. He knew what the letters said; he was just buying time until he was asked to leave. He probably had already been asked to leave; that's why he didn't open the letters.

After eating the best meal he had in months, Boots decided to head back home. He figured Coach had come and gone by now.

He had no heat or electricity, but since the apartments around him still had power, his room wasn't freezing cold. He still had to wear all of his clothes to bed to stay warm. The baloney and bread were gone, so he would be back on the street begging tomorrow.

He counted his money as he started home. He had eleven dollars and forty-three cents for a day of begging in the cold.

Boots was going to be glad to get home. He had stopped and bought a cheap sandwich at the corner grocery store and was planning on eating it as soon he got home.

He put the key in the door, and it didn't work. He tried once again, and it still didn't work. He realized that the locks had been changed. He knew this was coming, but he had thrown the letters from the booster in the garbage can. He really was homeless now.

The only thing he had besides the clothes on his back was his Olympic medal, which he carried wrapped up in a handkerchief. He knew the medal was expensive and valuable. He could get a lot of money for it, but he had put so much of his life into training to win it, he would rather die than part with it. He had reached his lowest point in his life. The only way out that he could see was to contact Mr. Longhurst and ask for a job, but he didn't even have money to get back to Mississippi. He remembered when he was in training less than a year ago, he would go on long runs all over the city. He remembered several times running past a homeless shelter not far away, and they had a big sign out front telling the homeless they could spend the cold nights in their shelter. Boots didn't know if that was still true, but he had nowhere to go, so he headed for the shelter.

When he got to the shelter, they asked him a lot of questions; one of the questions was his name. He didn't want anyone to recognize the name Boots, since it was an unusual name but had become popular just a few months ago after winning the Olympics, so he told them his real name, James Harris. He at least had a place to sleep and eat now.

In the meantime, since Coach Turner could not find Boots for Christmas dinner, he had started a search to find out what happened.

He went by the car lot and was told he had quit.

He checked at the university to see if he was enrolled—nothing.

Coach started asking people who were friends of Boots if they had seen him.

He told Coach Sines all that had happened, and he suggested checking the police stations.

Boots was supposed to fly to New York in a little over a month to accept his award, yet he couldn't be found.

Coach Sines had contacted one of the businessmen on the cards that Boots had given him, and he had him a job lined up but no Boots.

Two weeks had gone by, and one of the runners at UT told Coach Turner at practice that he saw a man begging that sort of looked like Booths over on Seventh Avenue.

"Are you sure?" the coach asked.

"No, I'm not sure, but he was the same height and same build as Boots. He had a beard, so it was hard to see his face, and I was running."

After practice, Coach headed toward Seventh Avenue and drove up and down the street several times. Nothing.

He told Coach Sines about what he had been told.

"I'll drive by there on the way to school tomorrow, and if I don't see anyone, you can drive by before practice starts tomorrow, and then I'll drive back by after practice, and we'll see if that was him."

"We've got to find him before the awards presentation. Can you imagine the announcer saying; 'And now the athlete of the year from the University of Tennessee,' and he's not even there?" Coach Turner asked.

For the next several days, the coaches took turns driving up and down Seventh Avenue but never saw anyone begging.

Since Coach Turner was also a pastor, he decided to check out the homeless shelter. He had often visited the homeless as part of his ministry.

He knew the shelters around Knoxville, so he decided to start with the one closest to where Boots had lived. He went in and asked the person in charge of the shelter if they had anyone named Boots Harris staying there.

The pastor was told no one by that name had been staying there.

As the coach started to leave, the person in charge said, "We do have a James Harris staying here."

It took a few seconds for the coach to realize that was Boots's real name.

"Is he here now?" the coach asked.

"I think so. He hasn't been feeling very well the last few days, as I recall."

The coach was led back to where Boots was sleeping. The coach bent over and looked at Boots's face while he was sleeping. He had grown a beard and looked ten years older than the last time he had seen him only a few weeks ago.

The coach turned to the manager and told him this was the man he had been looking for. He thanked him for his help.

The coach didn't want to startle Boots, so he quietly said, "Boots, it's Coach Turner." Boots didn't respond, so he touched his shoulder and said it again. This time, Boots opened his eyes. He thought he was dreaming at first.

Coach Turner told Boots to get his things; he was going home to stay with him. Boots told him he didn't have anything else.

Boots explained the other clothes he had were in the locked room where he used to live.

Coach let Boots do the talking on the way home. He didn't want to embarrass him anymore than he already was.

They stopped at a fast-food place on the way home, and Coach bought Boots some food to eat. He looked like he had lost ten pounds since he had seen him last.

While Boots took a shower and freshened up, coach's wife, Darlene, washed the clothes Boots had been wearing. When Boots finished cleaning up, the coach showed him the room he would be staying in and told Boots to lie down and rest while he and his wife went shopping for a few things. They had looked at his clothes sizes and were going out to buy him some more clothes.

When they got home with the clothes and a few groceries, Boots was still asleep. He slept until Coach knocked on the door and told him it was suppertime.

Coach Turner told Boots that Coach Sines had talked to one of the businessmen whose card Boots had given him, and he had offered Boots a job.

While out buying clothes and groceries, Coach Turner and his wife talked about how to best handle Boots living in their home. Coach wanted to make sure his wife agreed with Boots living there.

Coach told Boots he could live in the basement, in a room that had been built for his son, who had since moved away. He would be given a key, and he could come and go through the door attached to the basement room.

By winning the Olympics and now being named Track Athlete of the Year, he could use this fame to his advantage, but if people who wanted to provided endorsements and speaking engagements couldn't find him, he would just fade away, which was exactly what happened to him over the last few months.

When he would be awarded Track Athlete of the Year next month, it could lead to all kinds of business opportunities, but it had become obvious that Boots wasn't able to handle it the last time, so he needed to take advantage this time. It would probably be his last chance.

The following Monday, Boots rode to work with Coach Turner so he could meet with Coach Sines later and talk about the job he had lined up with Mr. Barnes.

Coach Sines talked to Boots for a while and then took him down to say a few words to the track team who were finishing up their indoor track season.

Boots talked to them about his training and workouts to prepare himself for making the Olympic team. He also told the team how lucky they were to have Coach Sines and Coach Turner coaching them. He told how they had sacrificed in their personal lives, both financially and time wise, to help him in his Olympic quest.

When he finished his talk, Coach Sines told him they were to meet Mr. Barnes for lunch to discuss possible job opportunities for Boots.

"What kind of business is Mr. Barnes in?" Boots asked.

"A little bit of everything," Coach replied. "But his biggest business is in the restaurant industry. He owns all the Burger Barnes in the area. He owns the restaurant we are meeting him at today—Barnes Steak and Seafood Restaurant."

Boots remembered the one time he ate a steak and how good it was. He hoped they might have steak today, but he figured they wouldn't. *It's too expensive*, he thought. Anything would be good compared to the food he had been getting at the homeless shelter.

When they pulled up in front of the restaurant, Coach got out of the car and handed a young man the keys. Boots had no clue why he hadn't just parked in the lot and why he was handing the keys to a stranger. He might just drive away in the car and never come back.

As they were walking up the steps, Boots asked Coach why he had given the keys to a strange man.

The coach had to explain valet parking to Boots. Coach said, "I told you this is an important man. He is also fair and won't treat you like that McCoy crook."

When they entered the restaurant, Boots marveled at the place; it looked more like a palace than a restaurant.

The person behind the stand told the coach that Mr. Barnes was expecting them and to follow him.

They were ushered into a private room with a large dining table. Boots had never seen a table that large. The room was decorated like they were in someone's dining room.

"I'll tell Mr. Barnes you are here," the man said.

"Classy, isn't it, Coach?" Boots asked.

Before he could answer, in walked Mr. Barnes. He shook Coach

Sines's hands and introduced himself to Boots before Coach had a chance to, even though they had meet at McCoy's party.

He told Boots he had followed him all the way through the Olympics and how proud he was of the way he had represented the University of Tennessee and his country.

"Let's order something to eat before we talk business. I'm starving," Mr. Barnes said. He motioned to a waiter who was standing outside the door. The waiter came in and took their drink orders and left.

"Guys, order anything on the menu. I know the owner, and he gives me a discount," he said, laughing.

Boots looked down at the menu and over at the prices beside each item; he couldn't believe it. There were things on the menu that cost close to fifty dollars.

He was looking at the cheapest things on the menu when Mr. Barnes said, "Boots, how about I order for you? Do you like steak and lobster?"

Boots had never tasted lobster, but he sure knew what steak tasted like. Boots said, "Yes, sir, I do."

Boots glanced down at the menu. It was the most expensive item on the menu.

When the waiter came back in, Mr. Barnes said, "The young gentleman and I will have the steak and lobster. What are you going to have, Coach?"

Coach Sines ordered the seafood platter.

"While we are waiting on our meals, Boots, let me tell you what I have planned for you. I know you have the awards ceremony coming up next month—and congratulations on that, by the way. I have several jobs that you could do, but I would like to start you out working here. You would be a door greeter like you saw when you came in. You would greet people as they come in and tell one of the waiters what table to take them to. There will be a little picture on the stand of all the tables, and you just put a number beside the people's names on the registry, and the waiter would take them to that table. When they have left and the table has been cleaned up, the waiter or waitress will tell you it is available for new customers. I know you want to go back to school and finish the two classes, so we can work around your schedule. You can work during the day or at night, depending on your school schedule.

"If that is not acceptable, we can find you a job in one of my fast-food restaurants, but I think that would be beneath your skills and being the famous athlete that you are. So, what do you think of my proposal?" Mr. Barnes asked.

Boots looked at Coach Sines.

"I told you he was a class act," Coach said.

Boots said, "That sounds great, Mr. Barnes. Thank you."

"Great. I think you will be happy here. If you could stop by sometime tomorrow or the next day and see Mr. Fisher, our manager, he will set you up with a suit like the one the door greeter was wearing when you came in. Oh, I guess we need to talk salary. I'm not sure what our door greeter's salary is, but I know it is well above minimum wage."

When the meals arrived, Boots took the first bite of steak, and it was even better than the one he had eaten several years ago. Boots had no clue what to do with that lobster tail, so he waited to see how Mr. Barnes ate his. *What a day*, he thought. *Sure better than that creep McCoy.*

As they were riding home, Coach asked him how he thought it had gone.

"I'm afraid I'll wake up tomorrow in the homeless shelter and all this was just a dream," he said. He thanked Coach again for all he had done to help him get to the Olympics and now to get a job. Begging on the street was cold and embarrassing to him.

As they were continuing to head back to the coaches' offices, Boots could not imagine how the day could get any better; he was about to find out it could.

When they walked into the coaches' offices, Coach Sines suggested they stop by and tell Coach Turner the good news.

After walking into the office, Coach Turner had some more good news. He had contacted the booster who had let Boots live in the apartment rent-free, and he had allowed Coach Turner to go over and get the clothes Boots had left behind when he was locked out. One of the things was the Olympic uniform he had worn in the opening and closing ceremonies during the Olympics.

Now Boots knew there was no way this day could get any better.

After eating at Coach Turner's, he went downstairs to his new—and he hoped temporary—home. He piled the few clothes in the corner that Coach Turner had gotten from his old apartment.

He looked at the uniform he had worn during the ceremonies and thought of how proud he was to represent his country, especially during the closing ceremonies when he was also wearing his goal medal.

He looked at the straw hat with the red, white, and blue ribbon around it, and it still looked stupid to him.

The following day, he caught the bus to meet the manager at the restaurant to get measured for his new uniform and to be shown how to greet people. He would start work the following Monday; he was looking forward to it and saying goodbye to homeless shelters forever. He thought if he ever became rich, he would go back and help that homeless shelter financially.

Boots was told that he could give the coach's phone number to certain people who were his friends, so he had given it to Larry. He received a call from Larry inviting him to the bar with his friends.

Boots didn't have enough money to go to the bar and drink. He had enough for maybe one beer, so he decided to drop by for one drink and then make an excuse why he had to leave early.

Coach Turner had given him enough tokens to ride the bus to some of the places he would need to go to get ready for his upcoming job, so he didn't have to pay for bus fare.

When he got to the bar, the three guys were already drinking. He sat down and began talking. He didn't order right away since he had enough money for only the one beer.

The waitress came over, and Larry ordered another beer and said, "Give my old buddy Boots a beer on me."

Boots thanked him; now he would be able to drink two before his money ran out.

Since they had not seen Boots in a long time, Skip and Bruce wanted him to catch them up on what was happening in his life.

He told them about the new job he would be starting on Monday.

"Wow, you're in with Mr. Barnes. That's big-time. You'll be rich in no time." Larry laughed.

Boots drank the beer Larry had bought him and ordered the one he could afford. He drank each one very slowly so he could stretch the time out with his friends. The other guys had drunk three while he was still nursing the one.

Boots finally came up with some excuse about having to help Coach Turner with something important, so he could leave. He hoped this was the last time he was not be able to afford a beer, now that he had a decent job.

The following Monday, Boots went to work, hopefully the start of a new life.

After he finished his first night at work, Coach Turner asked how he liked his new job.

Boots told the coach and his wife it really didn't seem like a job. He just greeted people and smiled. A few recognized him for his Olympic achievement and asked for pictures and autographs.

Boots sure liked signing autographs better than begging on the streets.

At the end of the week, he received his first paycheck, and it was almost twice what he had made working for Mr. McCoy. He also found out he got to eat a free meal, either before or after his shift.

The following week, Boots received his plane ticket to attend the ceremonies in New York. His coaches would be allowed to attend the banquet with him, which made him feel a lot better. He still hated to fly, and he knew nothing about big cities, so the coaches would help him find where he was supposed to go.

He and the coaches were shown around the city by some representatives of the New York Athletic Club. Boots had been to Rome, but it was nothing like this.

Boots had his name read as the Track Athlete of the Year for the year 1960. He thanked his coaches and his university for giving him the opportunity and also the New York Athletic Club, and as he finished, he held the trophy toward the sky and thanked his mother and father.

Following the ceremonies, Boots was bombarded by radio, TV, and newspaper interviews, just like he had been after the Olympics.

When they arrived back home, it was the same as in New York. It was like old times for Boots again; he was the hero of campus, the city, and the entire state.

His first night back at work, he was mobbed by his coworkers. Many hadn't known he was an Olympic champion, but now everyone knew it.

Mr. Barnes took a full page out in the local paper, showing Boots holding his medal and the trophy. He invited people to come by the restaurant and say hello to Boots.

When Boots saw the paper, he hoped this wasn't like the ploy Mr. McCoy had used. To his relief, it wasn't.

He did notice that a framed picture, the same one that was in the paper, was placed in the restaurant. Mr. Bryon never pressured Boots to promote the restaurant; all he asked of him was to be nice and friendly to the customers.

Boots didn't really have an address that anyone knew, since he was staying with Coach Turner. Most of his mail was being sent to the University of Tennessee's coaches. Coach Turner took the mail home to Boots.

Boots wasn't sure some of the letters were legit. He showed the coach a few of them. He was being offered all kinds of money for endorsements.

The coach told him he would call about some of the letters and see if they were for real.

The following day, Coach Sines had been out of the office most of the day, so when he came in, Coach Turner told him the news. He walked into Sines's office and closed the door.

He told him he had called about some of the endorsements Boots was being offered. It was unbelievable some of these offers. Wheaties was offering several thousand dollars if they could use his picture on their cereal boxes. He could also receive bonuses if the sales increased to a certain point.

Coach Sines said, "You're kidding. It's about time the kid receives what he deserves."

Boots was working the night shift, so it was late when he got home. He was surprised to see Coach and his wife waiting on him.

When the coach told him what he had found out, Boots thought he was kidding. He finally realized it was true.

The coach told him he needed someone like an accountant or maybe a lawyer to handle all of these things. Boots knew no one who was a lawyer or an accountant, but he trusted that what Coach suggested was true. He was still shocked about getting money for saying he liked someone's product.

Boots couldn't go to sleep for thinking of the money he would be getting. He didn't even have enough money a few weeks ago to buy two beers, and now he could be getting thousands of dollars.

He would be able to afford a place of his own, instead of having to mooch off of Coach Turner and his wife. He still didn't have a driver's license, so maybe he could actually get a car instead of taking the bus or begging for rides from people.

When he arrived at work the following day, the manager said he needed to report to Mr. Barnes's office before starting his shift.

Boots felt a sick feeling in his stomach; he wondered what he had done wrong. He didn't like being called into the boss's office. He remembered the last time that happened; he ended up taking his shirt off and throwing it in the floor and telling Mr. McCoy he quit. But Mr. Barnes had always been nice to him. He just wanted it over with.

He knocked on Mr. Barnes's door and heard someone tell him to come in.

He opened the door, and Mr. Barnes was on the phone and motioned for him to sit down.

Boots was nervous and hoped the conversation Mr. Barnes was having wouldn't take long.

Mr. Barnes finally hung up. He shook Boots's hand and asked how things were going.

It didn't look like he was in trouble, but he still wasn't sure. He remembered how nice McCoy could be sometimes, but it was just an act.

"Boots, I know you want to knock off those two courses that you lack at school. I was wondering when you want to take those classes. I was thinking you could go the first part of summer school and get them out of the way. We will work your schedule here around your classes."

Boots was caught off guard. Here the man was trying to help him instead of chewing him out for doing something wrong.

"That would be great," Boots replied. "I would like to finally graduate from college."

"Why don't you run by the university's admissions office sometime and pick up the paperwork, and we'll get the ball rolling," Mr. Barnes said.

Boots got up to leave. He turned to Mr. Barnes and told him how much he appreciated the help he had been.

"I'm here anytime you need me or have a problem," Mr. Barnes said.

Boots walked out of the office relieved; not only was it nothing bad, but it turned out to be something good.

Boots went by the university the following week to get the papers he needed. He thought he would stop by and see the coaches, but then he remembered they were at the SEC championships this week.

Coach had set him up with a lawyer to handle his endorsements. He went by the lawyer's office to talk to him, and he was told everything was a go on the Wheaties deal. All he had to do was sign the papers, and he would be getting his first check in a few weeks.

Boots knew that lawyers got part of the deal. He was just hoping to get enough money to finally move out of Coach's house; he had been imposing too long as it was.

A couple weeks passed, and Boots was working the afternoon shift. As he opened his basement door, he saw some letters in between the doors. Coach would usually bring the mail he received at school and just put it in the door. Even though he was living in Coach's house, there were days he didn't see Coach or his wife.

He went in and plopped down on the bed to look through his mail. He noticed a letter from Wheaties. He tore the letter open, and inside was a letter along with a check for $3,000.

He looked at the check several times. He couldn't believe it; he was rich. He jumped off the bed and started dancing around. *Is this really real?* he thought.

He needed to tell someone, but Coach wasn't home.

He decided to call Larry and see if he was home.

Larry answered, and he told him he had just gotten his first check from Wheaties and the beer was on him tonight. He told him to call Skip and Bruce and invite them too.

He didn't have to be at work until two the following day, so it was party time. He had not been so happy since the Olympics and the awards in New York.

Boots knew it was too late to go to the bank, so he hid the check with his goal medal. He had enough money from his work to cover the bar bill later. This was going to be a night to remember, he thought as he walked out the door.

He almost decided to call a cab, since he was now rich, but he decided to walk to the bus stop and wait for the bus. He had told Larry to meet him at six, and it was only a little after five.

When all the guys had arrived, he told them about his deal with Wheaties, but he didn't tell them how much the check he had received was for.

Boots was relatively new to the drinking game, whereas the other three were seasoned veterans. Boots had been drunk once in his life, so he drank his beer a lot slower than the other guys. The other guys, on the other hand, were drinking three to one of Boots's since he was buying.

They had been drinking for several hours when Larry suggested they go to another bar where the action was a lot better than this sleepy bar. Everyone was ready, except Boots. He was ready to go home, but they kept insisting.

The other three could barely walk to the car, so Larry threw Boots the keys and told him to drive.

Boots didn't want the guys to know he had no driver's license and his total time behind a car had been moving the one car he sold around to the shop, about a total of one hundred yards.

Boots couldn't remember how many beers he had, but it was not as many as the time he had drank and gotten sick.

He reluctantly got behind wheel. There wasn't a lot of traffic on the road, so he shouldn't have any problem keeping the car in between two white lines. He would just drive slowly; it wasn't like he was going to have to parallel park or anything.

They had driven a couple of miles, and Boots was gaining more confidence in his driving; this wasn't so bad. He had never driven a car at night, but the streetlights lit the road up so he could see the oncoming traffic well.

Larry said, "Speed up. You drive like an old woman."

Boots didn't notice that they were about to run into a section of road that had no streetlights.

He stepped down on the gas pedal and turned to ask Larry if he was driving fast enough now.

When Boots woke up, he was in the hospital. He had no clue what had happened.

He was later told that he had moved out of his lane and hit an oncoming car head-on. He was also told that an elderly woman had been killed. He would be charged with drunk driving, driving without a license, drug possession, and involuntary manslaughter.

Boots drifted off to sleep because of all the medication he was on. When he awoke a few hours later, he hoped that what he remembered was a nightmare; it wasn't.

He didn't know it at the time, but Larry's car contained lots of drugs. It seemed that after Larry quit McCoy's, he began a new job as a drug dealer.

Boots had several broken bones, including his left leg and left arm. He would be treated for several days and then sent to jail awaiting his trial.

He had started out his life on the bottom, moved to the top, and was back on the bottom. With the newly found success with the endorsements, it seemed like he was back on top again; now he could not be any more on the bottom than he was.

Since he basically had no money, a public defender was assigned to his case. He hadn't even gotten to cash his Wheaties check. All those deals were down the drain now.

He was facing prison time, but how much was the question. He also had to deal with the fact that he was responsible for someone's death.

Boots went before a judge, and his bond was set at $20,000. Boots had nothing; he probably wouldn't make that much in the next ten years, so jail was going to be his new home until the trial.

The public defender came in and questioned Boots. He knew the lawyer was just going through the motions to earn his salary. Boots told him he knew nothing about the drugs in the car, but he acted like he didn't even hear it.

The following week, Boots was taken into a room with handcuffs on. The guard stayed outside the room. In a few minutes, a man dressed in a suit walked in and introduced himself as Mr. Mason, Boots's new lawyer.

Boots didn't know what was going on. He asked what happened to the other lawyer, but he didn't receive an answer at first.

The lawyer started asking Boots to describe what happened the night of the accident.

Boots asked again what happened to the other lawyer.

"Mr. Harris, I have been hired to represent you by someone who wants to remain anonymous. You would have no chance with the lawyer that was appointed for you. I am not saying I can keep you out of prison, because I probably can't, but I am a good lawyer and can probably get your sentence reduced if you will cooperate with me. We will build up the fact that you have never been in trouble with the law and are someone who is respected worldwide by the athletic community. Now, will you please answer a few questions for me?"

Boots told him what happened that evening and that he did not know that Larry was a drug dealer or that there were any drugs in the car.

"Why do you not have a driver's license?" the lawyer asked.

Boot explained that he never had anyone who would teach him to drive, and he was too ashamed to ask anyone.

"So, we will play the fact that you didn't want to drive to start with and you had no clue about the drugs. Can anyone prove how many beers you drank that night?" he asked.

"I don't think so," Boots replied.

"So, how many did you have?" Mr. Mason asked. "Off the record of course."

"I had four I think," Boots replied.

"I don't need you to think; I need to know," Mason replied.

"It was four. I was going to order another, when Larry suggested we go somewhere else."

"So you said you entered a section where the streetlights ran out. Is that correct?" he asked.

"Yes," Boots replied.

"Were the lights of the oncoming car on bright or dim?"

"I don't know," Boots replied.

"Did they seem brighter than most of the cars coming toward you?" Mason asked.

"I think so," Boots replied.

"Do you wear glasses?"

"No," Boots replied.

"Have you ever had your eyes checked for glasses?" the lawyer asked.

"No," Boots answered.

"So, do you think you have perfect vision?" he asked.

"I don't guess," Boots answered. He wasn't sure what perfect vision was.

"Good. I think I can build a pretty good case from the information you have given me. Just don't expect miracles," he said as he walked out the door.

It would be several weeks before Boots would hear from his lawyer again. In the meantime, he was locked up in a jail cell and eating food like he had received in the homeless shelter.

Boots did not have any visitors while he was locked up. He knew he had let everyone down. Seemed like there was no in between; he was either on top or on the bottom. It looked like this would be the final thing that would keep him on the bottom.

The following week, he had another visit with Mr. Mason. He went over the defense he had prepared and told Boots under no circumstances would he be allowed to take the stand. He also told him that what he had done was a felony and he would probably have to serve some time in the state prison; he just didn't know how much time.

Boots was afraid to ask, but he did anyway. "How much time are we talking about?"

"From one to five years. I'm hoping to get you off with two, but it depends on the judge," Mr. Mason said.

Boots sat with his head down, trying to envision spending two years in prison.

He knew when he got out, no one would want to hire an ex-con, so he would have to beg for money again.

Boots had never been on a date in his life, but he had dreamed of someday getting married and having children. He could see himself coming home from work and helping his young son train to make the high school track team, telling him about the time he was an Olympic champion and showing him his gold medal. Boots now knew this dream would never happen.

He remembered how Coach Turner kept telling him that this life meant nothing and where you spend eternity was all that mattered. He could change or live another fifty years like he had lived up to this point—a failure.

Boots would have to return to the hospital for a couple more visits before being transferred to his new home, a jail cell.

He was given the details surrounding the accident. Larry, Skip, and Bruce all had drugs in their system when brought to the hospital. Each had minor injuries and was released from the hospital. They would face drug charges, Larry receiving the most, since he owned the car where the drugs were found. They all would get off with slaps on the wrists compared to Boots.

The woman who was killed in the crash was in her eighties, and her husband, who was also in the car, received some injuries and had to spend a few days in the hospital recovering.

Just before being transferred to jail, Coach Turner showed up at the hospital. He and Coach Sines had been attending the SEC outdoor championships in Florida.

Coach Turner tried to stay positive and cheer Boots up, but they both knew this was not going to turn out well.

Coach Turner, speaking as a pastor now, told Boots once again this life is not what really matters. He could still turn his life for the better by giving his life to the Lord.

As had been Boots's excuse all along, he thought, *Let me get through this trial, and then I'll think about accepting the Lord.*

He was transported to the county jail. He was in a wheelchair because, with a broken leg and arm, he couldn't use crutches yet.

As the bars slammed shut behind him, he faced the reality that it probably would be years before he ever got out. He was now at his lowest point, and a deep depression set in.

He lay on his bunk thinking of when he stepped to the top of the podium and had that gold medal placed around his neck. He was on top of the world, and now he couldn't sink any lower. He even longed for the days he was living in the homeless shelter; it was better than this.

The following week, he met with his lawyer again and was told that they would be going to a hearing the following Friday.

Mr. Mason told him he would ask for the charges to be dropped because it was an accident and he had no prior records, but he was also told the judge would deny his request because of the alcohol involved.

"I'm going to ask for a jury trial because whoever they would get to serve on the jury has surely heard of you as a result of your Olympic success, and they would feel more compassionate toward you than if the judge were the deciding one. Plus, most of the jury probably have been out drinking before and can see the same thing might have happened to them. They would look on it as more of an accident than you drinking too much. But I must warn you, the judge will probably deny my request for a trial by jury. It would be hard to find enough jurors who did not know about your past success in the Olympics."

The judge did exactly what the lawyer had expected during the pretrial; he denied the motions. The case would be tried the following month.

Mr. Mason sat with Boots and discussed the day's events.

"I didn't expect the judge to grant either of my requests," Mr. Mason said. "We have a month to prepare your defense. Again, don't expect to get off without any prison time. I'm shooting for two years or less, but that is not a guarantee. Remember, you were drinking, had no license, and someone was killed. I'm not a miracle worker, but we will give you the best defense possible."

Boots was taken back to his jail cell. He had always thought that people in jail were criminals and deserved to be there. But now that he was a prisoner in jail, he realized that all it took to put someone behind bars was doing something stupid like he had done.

The hardest thing to adjust to was the fact that he was behind bars and all of his privileges and choices were taken away from him. He did what he was told to do and when he was told. He felt like a four-year-old kid being told everything to do by his parents.

The homeless shelter was looking better every day.

A few weeks later, Boots was escorted into the courtroom in a new suit and tie that had been provided by his lawyer's assistant. He had no idea who was paying for the lawyer or the clothes.

The bailiff told everyone to rise as the judge entered the courtroom.

Mr. Mason addressed the judge. "Your Honor, we have a young man sitting before this court today who is a model citizen. He has been admired inspiration to not only this city but all over the world for his athletic achievements and his outstanding character.

"He was involved in an automobile accident that was tragic. There were circumstances that contributed to this tragedy. He entered an area that had no streetlights, and his eyes were adjusting to the darkness, when all of a sudden a car approached with its headlights on bright, and he momentarily crossed a few feet over the center line.

"This is truly regrettable, but it could happen to anyone. It would be a tragedy for this young man to be sent to prison, when he could affect so many people by sharing his story to motivate people to be more careful while driving.

"So, Your Honor, we ask that the court drop the charges and instead have him serve a probationary period in which he is to give his story to certain groups around the city.

"Thank you, Your Honor, for hearing our request."

"I object, Your Honor," said the prosecuting attorney. "The fact that Mr. Hines is a well-known athlete has nothing to do with the fact that he willfully decided to get behind the wheel of a car, after drinking in a bar, and driving without a license, causing the death of an innocent woman. He also caused injuries to this fine woman's husband. He has lost a wife and a lifelong companion because of Mr. Hines's negligence and disregard for human life. We ask that Mr. Mason's request be denied. It would be a travesty of justice to let this man go free. Thank you, Your Honor."

"Mr. Mason, I tend to agree with the prosecuting attorney, Mr. Fish, so I am denying your request to drop the charges against Mr. Hines. Mr. Hines will be tried before this court. You may present your opening statements, even though it seems like we just did that," the judge grumbled.

Boots had never seen what went on in a courtroom before, so he had no clue what to expect.

The lawyers went over all the events leading up to Boots and his friends getting into the car.

The bartender was called in to testify about how many drinks Boots had before he left the bar.

The judge banged his gavel down and pronounced court adjourned until after lunch.

Before they left the courtroom, Mr. Mason told Boots things had gone exactly as he had expected.

After lunch, court resumed, and the events leading up to the accident were presented. Boots sat there listening to all that was being said, and he knew it didn't look good.

Later that night, while lying on his cot in his jail cell, Boots realized that the trial had started on the same day he had been scheduled to start summer school. It now appeared he would be going to prison and never graduate from college.

The lawyers presented their closing arguments before the court and the judge ruled as everyone expected—guilty. Boots had been drinking, he had no driver's license, and he had caused a death in the accident.

Boots and Mr. Mason now stood before the judge for sentencing. He could receive one to five years in the state prison. Mr. Mason had told him he was hoping to get the sentence down to two years, but he wasn't sure that would happen.

The judge said, "Mr. Harris, you are hereby sentenced to spend one year in the state penitentiary in Nashville, Tennessee. The court hopes during that time period you will realize you don't drink and drive without a license."

Before he was taken back to jail, Boots once again asked Mr. Mason who had hired him.

"I don't guess it makes any difference if you know now. Mr. Longhurst hired me."

Boots was shocked; he thought it would have been a big booster or businessman in Knoxville. *Why would Mr. Longhurst do that?* he wondered.

Lying on his cot that night, he went over the day's events in his head. He knew he would be found guilty, because he was. He was surprised at getting only a one-year sentence. He was not looking forward to going to prison because of all the stories he had heard about prison life. A local jail was bad enough, but prison was a different story.

He had been to Nashville for a few track meets, and he loved listening to country music, but he never thought he would be back there, this time in prison.

Boots was set to be transferred to the Tennessee State Prison in Nashville the following day. Before he left, Coach Turner stopped by to talk with him about his future.

"Ever since you come to UT, I have been telling you about what is important in this life. You have always put off the decision, claiming something else is more important at the moment. Where would you be right now if you had been the one who died in that car accident? You would be spending eternity in the torment of hell. What you are going through right now will be like paradise compared to an eternity in hell.

"Your goal in life was to win a gold medal. You, like most people, strive for the riches and gold of this life. If I were to ask you what your greatest accomplishment in life has been, you would undoubtedly say winning the goal medal in the Olympics.

"When you die, you can't take that medal with you. When this earth is destroyed—and it will be by Jesus someday—that medal will fade away.

"If you become saved and live with Jesus in heaven, gold will be so common in heaven that you will be walking on streets made of gold, and it will never fade away.

"I'll try to come and visit you when we are in the Nashville area for track meets or if we are there recruiting, but while you are there, you need to decide where you want to spend eternity. I'll write you when I get your address. Remember, I love you, and so does God."

The following day, Boots was transported to the state prison. He was scared. He was taken to his new home for the next year. He couldn't believe how big the prison was. He knew there were murders and all kinds of deranged men incarcerated inside these walls. He hoped his roommate was not one of these.

When he arrived at his cell, he was surprised it was empty. He saw there were items near the other cot that belonged to someone, so he knew he was not going to be in the cell alone.

He sat down on the cot as the officer removed his leg irons and handcuffs. As the officer walked out the door, the bars slammed behind him; prison life had now begun.

In a little while, the bars opened, and in walked his new roommate. He was a medium-size man who looked like he had lived a rough life. He was covered in tattoos and had several scars on his face.

"New roomy, I see," the man said. "Just call me Rocky. And you are?"

"James," Boots replied.

Boots didn't want anyone to know about his past or that people called him Boots.

He had been proud of winning the Olympic gold medal, but now he was ashamed to let people know he was a champion who was in prison for causing someone's death. He knew that now that he was a convicted felon, he would never be looked at in the same light that he was when he was the 1,500-meter champion of the Olympics.

Rocky asked Boots what he was in for, and Boots told him the whole story.

"Bummer," Rocky said.

Rocky was in for robbery and assault.

Boots asked Rocky about the prison, and he was told to watch his back and not to trust anyone.

Boots received his first letter from Coach Turner. He told him about the track team and how they should be able to compete for the SEC championships this year. Most of the letter had nothing to do with him being in prison. He told him to take care of himself and watch out for the leeches; they were everywhere. He told him his gold medal was locked up in a safe place, not to worry. The last line of the letter said that Mr. Longhurst had died.

Tears began to fill Boots's eyes. The man who had done so much for his family and him was now gone.

Boots knew if it hadn't been for this man hiring a first-class lawyer, he would be spending several more years behind these bars. He couldn't even attend his funeral.

He had planned on asking Mr. Longhurst for a job working in the cotton fields when he got out of prison. He knew no one in Knoxville would hire him after what he had done. His parents' belongings were still stored in a shed on Mr. Longhurst's plantation, so he had accepted that as his future. But now that Longhurst had died, he didn't know what he would do when he got out.

Boots spent the first few days not saying much to anyone. He knew there was an adjustment period for all new inmates, and you had to find your niche and stay away from the really bad people.

Rocky worked in the laundry and told Boots he needed to apply for a job. It at least got you out of your cell for a few hours.

Boots applied for a job and was assigned to the part of the prison that made license plates. Making license plates for the state of Tennessee drew in big bucks for the prison.

As time went by, Boots found out that Rocky had grown up without a father, and he had seven brothers and sisters. His mother worked at odd jobs but could never keep a job for very long because of her drug use. She lived for the first of the month when she received a check, but it was usually gone before half of the month was over. Rocky had to steal and deal on the streets just to survive. He had dropped out of school after the eighth grade.

Rocky seemed like a good person, but he had to fight for everything he had ever gotten, so he also had a tough, mean side too.

When Rocky asked Boots about his past, he told him about growing up on a plantation and picking cotton. He never told him he was an Olympic champion. It seemed he would be bragging, and he didn't want Rocky to think he was better than him. Boots didn't want to remember his past; he had been on top of the world, and now look where he was.

Boots witnessed many fights and even a stabbing his first two weeks in prison. He learned there were people to stay away from and tried to talk to as few people as possible.

Boots had noticed that Rocky was allowed to leave his cell the first two Sundays Boots was in prison; he decided to ask him where he went.

Rocky told Boots he attended church services to get out of his cell for an hour on Sundays. He told him he didn't believe in God, but at least it was a break from the prison cell. Rocky told him he should go too.

The following Sunday, they entered the area where the church services were held.

The pastor was at the door greeting the prisoners as they walked in. He said hello to Rocky and asked who this was he had with him.

Rocky said, "This is my new roomy, James."

The pastor reached out and shook James's hand and said, "It is a pleasure to meet you. I've never met an Olympic champion before. I never knew your name was James; I had always just heard you called Boots.

"I followed you in the newspaper through all your races. I saw you on the television as you were carrying the American flag around after you won the race. It made me proud to be an American."

Rocky looked at Boots like he had just seen a ghost. He wondered what was going on. He thought the pastor might have James mixed up with someone else. What would an Olympic champion be doing in prison? he wondered.

When James didn't deny what the pastor had said, he knew it must be true.

After returning to their cell, Rocky asked James what was going on and why he hadn't told him about his past.

"I'm a convicted felon who killed someone; my past is not important anymore. I didn't want anyone to know about my past. I didn't want people to think I am better than they are just because I won a stupid race. My life is forever ruined now, and the less people know about me, the better; if people knew, they would just want to ask me all kinds of questions."

"Since we are going to be in here together for a long time, you can just accept that I am going to ask you a lot of questions. I've never known anyone famous before."

"I used to be famous, but now all I'm famous for is killing someone and blowing the opportunity of making a lot of money and having a successful life."

Later that day, Rocky said, "I've been thinking, and I'm not sure it is wise for people in here to know about your past. A lot of guys would like to be around an Olympic champion so they could brag about being your friend to people back home. But there are also a lot of weird guys in here who would like to harm you or even kill you so they could brag about that also. You need to be careful."

"How would the pastor know who I was?" Boots asked.

"He can see the records of everyone in the prison. He may have heard it from the guards or even the warden. I'm sure not many prisons have a famous Olympic champion in their prison. So, if he knows, that means others know too," Rocky said.

"You probably should talk to the pastor next Sunday and see what he tells you. You also might need to tell him you don't want people to know who you are. I'll continue to call you James until you find out something."

"Thanks. I haven't been called James since I was in the eighth grade."

"How did you get the name Boots?"

Boots explained the whole story to Rocky. He had told his story hundreds of times, even on radio and TV, but this was the first time he had ever told it from behind bars.

The following Sunday, Boots asked the pastor if he could talk to him a few minutes after the service.

The pastor cleared it with the guards for Boots to stay a little longer than the normal service.

When Boots finally got back to his cell, Rocky couldn't wait to hear what the pastor had told him.

"It's not good," Boots said. "The pastor said all the guards, the warden, and workers at the prison know who I am. He told me that it was big news in the Nashville paper when I arrived, so he was sure that a lot of prisoners know too. He even told me he was going to ask me to speak at the church service some Sunday. I told him no, of course. I'm no church speaker. I don't even believe in God."

He knew that last part wasn't true, but he didn't want to look weak in front of Rocky. He was surprised he had even said that.

Coach Turner had been telling him for years he needed to accept the Lord. He knew he probably needed to, but he had always put it off because of something else going on at the time. That's was one thing he was going to have a lot of now—time.

Boots had never noticed until today, but as he walked through the chow line to get his food, a lot of prisoners were pointing and looking at him. It seemed his secret was not really a secret like he had hoped.

Rocky began to hear comments about the running star that was in prison. Some of the comments he heard had him worried about James's future. There were lots of men who were in prison for life with no chance of parole, and doing something to a famous person was like adding a knock to their gun. They could brag about being the one who took the Olympian down.

Boots had written Coach Turner a return letter, asking him to send him the address of Mrs. Longhurst so he could tell her how much he liked and appreciated how her husband had helped him. It had been over a month, and he had not heard from Coach. He knew the cross-country season was underway and figured that was why he had not heard from him.

Boots had completed two months of his twelve-month sentence. It seemed like he had been in prison for years. He was told when to eat, when to go to work, when he could shower, and when he could go out into the yard; he felt like a robot.

After finishing his shift at the license plate shop, he returned to his cell to find a letter lying on his bunk. He looked at the postmark, and it said Knoxville, Tennessee. *Probably from Coach*, he thought. But when he looked at the return address, it was from Mrs. Turner. Why would she be writing him?

Boots sat down on the cot and opened the letter. He couldn't believe what he read. Coach Turner had died. It seemed he had a heart problem that he had kept from everyone, including his wife, for years. He died of a massive heart attack. Tears began to roll down Boots's face. This man had done more to help Boots than anyone ever had.

The cell door opened, and in walked Rocky from his job at the laundry. He asked Boots what was wrong when he saw the tears on his face.

Boots shook his head; he couldn't even answer him. Finally he told Rocky that the closest thing to a father to him had died.

Rocky said, "I'm sorry, bro." He left Boots to his thoughts.

Boots read the rest of the letter, in which Mrs. Turner told him how proud her husband was of him. "He still thought you could make something important out of your life if you come to know the Lord." She went on to say that they had talked about this many times, but the night before he died, he told her once again how special Boots was.

Boots began to cry again. He didn't want Rocky to see him crying, but he couldn't stop.

Boots spent the rest of the week knowing what he had to do. He kept thinking of all the things Coach Turner had said.

He knew his life on earth was now ruined. He had been on top of the world, Olympic champion and Track Athlete of the Year, but now he was at rock bottom.

He didn't know how bad his fall had been reported by the news media, but he knew it had destroyed his reputation beyond repair. In the past, people couldn't wait to speak to him and have their picture taken or an autograph. He was stared at everywhere he went by people who looked up to him for his accomplishments, and now he was in a prison cell. He had no family, no paying job, and no hope for things getting better in the future. He was twenty-three years old, and his life had been destroyed.

Boots lay awake at night and even considered suicide. He wasn't sure how to do it from inside a prison cell. He believed in God and in hell. He knew if he was going to commit suicide, he needed to be saved before he took his life, but he didn't know how God felt about people who committed suicide. He hoped if he took his own life, he would still go to heaven, but he wasn't sure.

Boots left the cafeteria and headed to the license plate shop. The work was hard and boring, but at least it got him out of his cell.

One of the few people in prison, other than Rocky, that he considered his friend was George.

George knew the story about Boots's past, but he never said anything to Boots, and he still called him James.

They had worked at the same machine together since Boots had entered prison. George would get the different numbers ready or the license plate, and Rocky would press the numbers into the plate. George would hand him a new set of numbers, and the next plate would be stamped.

Guards were stationed all around the plate shop, and each prisoner was strip-searched before they were allowed to leave the building.

There was lots of noise around the room, so it was hard for anyone that wasn't really close to each other to hear.

George said to Boots, "Go to the infirmary tomorrow and tell them you're sick. Don't come in to work."

"What? Why?" Boots asked.

Just then, a guard came strolling by.

"I said, doesn't it seem hotter than normal in here?" George said.

After the guard was out of hearing range, George said, "Don't come to work tomorrow. I've heard that Catfish is going to try and hurt you tomorrow."

Catfish worked across the room on another machine. He was covered in tattoos and had no front teeth. He was in for killing two people in a bar fight several years ago.

Boots turned to look at Catfish, and George grabbed his arm and told him not to turn around.

"Are you sure?" Boots asked. "Why would he want to hurt me?"

"You're famous," George replied. "It would be another feather in his cap. Don't come to work tomorrow, I tell you," George repeated.

After eating and getting back to his cell, Boots lay there on his cot trying to figure out what to do.

Rocky asked Boots why he was so quiet. Boots finally told him what he had heard.

"Then don't go," Rocky replied.

"But I have to go back sometime. If I don't go tomorrow, he will just wait until I come back and do it then."

"Just don't turn your back on him then."

"But I have to; he works on a bench behind me. I can't keep turning around and looking at him."

Boots didn't sleep much that night, but he knew he had to go to work the next day. He had no clue what he was going to do or how he could protect himself, but he knew he had to go to work.

After breakfast, where Boots ate very little, he headed to the plate shop.

As he walked to his machine, George said in a nervous voice, "What are you doing here?"

"I can't play sick every day; might as well get it over with."

The morning went like every other morning. *Maybe George was wrong*, Boots thought.

After lunch, things were still going as normal. George got up to go get another load of plates to be lettered and numbered. Boots was finishing the stack of plates George had just laid on the table.

Boots was putting a plate in the machine and was ready to pull the press down and stamp the plate with the number. He didn't notice Catfish heading toward him.

Catfish was carrying an empty box toward the trash can. George had just loaded a dolly full of new plates and started back to his station when he saw Catfish. He saw Catfish pull a shank from underneath the box and raise it behind Boots's back. In a panic, he turned the dolly over, spilling the load of plates on the floor. It made a loud racket, which caused the guards to look in his direction. As the guards turned, they saw Catfish raising the shank behind Boots. One of the guards yelled at him to stop. Catfish look toward the guard but started down with the shank. Another guard lunged at Catfish with the butt of his rifle. He struck Catfish on the side of his head but not before Catfish had stabbed Boots with the shank.

Catfish was wrestled to the ground and sprayed with mace. He was handcuffed and taken to lockup.

Boots was rushed to the emergency center. Luckily, it had missed arteries and vital organs.

Boots knew he probably owed his life to George.

He also remembered what Coach Turner had been telling him.

He thought, *What if I had died? Where would I be spending eternity?*

He was able to return to his cell a few days later. After a week of struggling with the decision, he decided to give his life to Christ. It was in the middle of the night, and Rocky was asleep across the room. Boots slide off his cot onto his knees and put his elbows on his bed. He bowed his head and asked God to forgive him for his sins and become his Lord and Savior. Boots felt a peace he had never felt before, even though he was in prison.

He hoped he could pass on the way he felt to Rocky.

Church services the following morning seemed to have a new meaning. He listened to every word the chaplain said. After the service, he told the chaplain about accepting the Lord. The chaplain said a prayer with Boots and told him he would be contacting him during the week to help guide him on things he needed to do.

The following day after each had finished their job and eaten, Boots told Rocky what he had done. He wasn't sure how Rocky would react. To his surprise, Rocky told him he envied what he had done. He told Rocky he could do the same thing, but Rocky said he was too fixed in his ways to change now.

As he lay in his bed that night, Boots felt a relief he had never felt before. Even though he knew his life here on earth would never be the way it once was, he somehow felt peace, knowing that the Lord would take care of him.

Before dropping off to sleep, he had another thought: he would see his mother, father, and Coach Turner once again in heaven. He had the most peaceful night's sleep that he could ever remember.

A few weeks later, he received another letter from Ms. Turner telling him that her son, whom Boots had never met, was appointed the new pastor at their church. Boots didn't even know that their son was a pastor too.

Boots couldn't wait to write her back and tell her the good news about accepting God. He concluded the letter by telling her he would see Coach Turner again.

In the past, he had thought of suicide, but that thought had now drifted from Boots's mind. He didn't know why, but he had hope for his future. He had only a few more months left of his sentence. He had no idea where he would live or find a job when he got out, but he now had peace that God would provide.

Rocky noticed over the next few months a major change in Boots. He seemed happy and looked forward to getting out at the end of next month. Rocky still had another two years to serve before his parole hearing came up. Boots had tried to convince him that he needed to accept the Lord, but Rocky had lived this way all his life and wasn't interested in this God business.

Boots received another letter from Mrs. Tuner, and in it, she explained that before Bob died, they had talked about Boots coming back and living in the basement like he had before; they both agreed it was what they wanted to do for Boots. She went on to say, now that Bob had died, she still wanted to do what they had agreed on and let him stay in the basement.

She went on to say that Trevor had moved back in town with his family to pastor the church and that he would try to help Boots find a job.

Boots hated to impose on Mrs. Turner, but he felt like this was an answer to part of his prayers; he now had somewhere to live. He also knew he still had some true friends who had not held what he had done against him and were still willing to help him get back on his feet.

Boots wrote a return letter thanking Mrs. Turner for her kindness. He would do his best to help her in any way he could and would pay rent when he got a job. He assured her he would stay only until he could afford a place of his own.

The big day finally arrived, and Boots was released from prison. He had received fifty cents a day for working in the license plate shop. He had spent very little, so he hoped he would have enough money to buy a bus ticket back to Knoxville.

It was several miles into Nashville and the bus station. He knew he couldn't afford a cab, so he would walk and thumb his way into Nashville. After buying his bus ticket, he had fifteen dollars left.

He had eaten breakfast at the prison before he left, so he decided not to spend any money on food the rest of the day.

He had mailed Mrs. Turner and told her the day of his release, and she and her son were to pick him up when he arrived in Knoxville. He hoped he could use a phone at the bus station without having to pay for it; money was tight.

When he arrived in Knoxville, he had to get some change to use a pay phone. He was down to fourteen dollars and change.

Boots sat in the bus station for about thirty minutes, waiting on Mrs. Turner and her son, Trevor, to show up.

Finally, he saw Mrs. Turner and her son walking into the bus station. She put her arms around Boots and gave him a big hug and told him she missed him. He couldn't remember the last time anyone had hugged him. She then introduced him to Trevor. Boots couldn't believe how much he looked like his father.

On the ride home, Trevor asked Boots a lot about his Olympic experience and didn't mention his jail time.

It had been a long time since he had seen the city of Knoxville. He remembered all the good times he had while running at the University of Tennessee. He hadn't received a letter from Coach Sines, but while Coach Turner was still alive and writing him, he would say that Coach Sines said hello.

They pulled into the driveway, and Boots saw Coach Turner's old car sitting there. He had ridden many times in that car, going to track and cross-country meets. He was surprised Mrs. Turner kept it after he died.

As they entered the house, Mrs. Turner said, "Supper will be ready in about an hour. You boys go in and relax. You can put your things in your room in the basement; everything is still the same as when you left."

Trevor told Boots that his wife and two kids were out of town visiting her mother, so he would be eating with them tonight.

Boots went downstairs and put what few things he had on the bed. He sat down, remembering that the last time he sat on the bed, the accident hadn't happened. He still had a job, and things were starting to look up in his life, but then he went to the bar, and his life changed forever.

He went back upstairs, and Mrs. Turner was in the kitchen, preparing food. Trevor was sitting on the couch, watching TV.

Trevor got up and turned the TV off. He asked Boots what it was like in prison.

Boots said it was a terrifying experience, but he had a good cellmate, and he tried to stay to himself as much as possible.

Trevor said, "Mom told me you came to know the Lord while in prison."

Boots explained how Trevor's father had been after him since he first came to the university to give his life to Christ. Boots told him he had always believed in God but just kept putting the decision off because he had other things going on.

Boots told him how Trevor's father had talked with him the day before he left for prison about what if he had been the one who died in the car crash. "I had a lot of time to think while in prison, and I had run out of excuses for putting the decision off. I had been on top of the track world, had a new job, and your parents were letting me stay in your old room in the basement rent-free, and then I had to go to the bar and was dumb enough to get behind the wheel of a car, not knowing how to drive and having no driver's license and killing an innocent person. How stupid could I be?"

Trevor said, "That is an amazing story. You need to tell people that story. It shows that if you give your life to God, he can bring you out of the worst situations."

About that time, they heard Mrs. Turner calling from the kitchen that supper was ready. Boots was especially hungry since he hadn't eaten all day. His stomach had been growling for hours.

When they sat down to eat, Trevor bowed his head and said grace. Boots had never said grace before eating. He didn't want his fellow prisoners to see him, so he had just started eating. He realized he still had a lot to learn about being a Christian.

Boots couldn't remember when a meal had tasted so good. He had been eating prison and jail food for over a year, and it just barely qualified as food as far as he was concerned.

After supper, he and Trevor went into the living room, while Mrs. Turner cleaned up the kitchen. As they were sitting there, Trevor asked where his gold medal was, saying he would like to see it.

Boots told him he didn't know where it was; he hadn't seen it in well over a year. The night of the accident, he was arrested and taken directly to jail, and he didn't remember where the medal was.

Trevor walked into the kitchen and asked his mom if she knew where Boots's gold medal was.

She walked into the living room, still wiping her hands dry from doing the dishes, and said, "We locked it up in the safe over there behind that picture."

"Open it up. I'd like to see what a gold medal looks like," Trevor said.

"I don't even remember what the combination is," his mother said. "I'll have to go back in the office and see if I can find it."

It was more than ten minutes before she came back with the combination.

Trevor took the picture covering the wall safe off the wall and laid it in a chair.

His mother handed him the combination, and he carefully turned the dial in front of the safe. He gave it a tug, but it didn't open. He tried it a second time, and this time it opened.

His mother said, "It's wrapped up in that handkerchief."

Trevor reached into the safe and carefully took out the handkerchief and handed it to Boots.

This was the first time in almost a year and a half that Boots had seen or held his medal. He folded back the cloth and looked at his medal. He took it out and handed it to Trevor.

Trevor said, "Wow. Do you know how rare it is to even see one of these, much less hold it?"

Boots didn't respond, but he remembered what Trevor's father had told him, that one day he would be walking on streets made of gold.

Trevor said his goodbyes and told Boots he hoped to see him in church the following morning. Boots promised he would be there.

Trevor's mother said Boots would be attending with her, and they would see him in the morning.

That night, Boots slept in a normal bed for the first time in almost a year and a half. He was used to getting up at four thirty in the prison, so he was wide awake before he heard Mrs. Turner upstairs.

They ate breakfast and started out the door, heading for church. She said, "Here are the keys. Why don't you drive?"

Boots remembered what happened the last time someone gave him car keys and told him to drive. He explained to Mrs. Turner that he still didn't have a driver's license and didn't know how to drive. He was nearing his twenty-fifth birthday.

"We need to take care of that. Your driving lesson will start tomorrow," she said.

During the church service, he noticed a lot of people staring at him; some he remembered, and some he didn't. He had attended this church while on the track team, since it was a requirement of Coach Sines that all the athletes attended somewhere. He had come to know many of the congregation, and he remembered they had taken up an offering so his parents could attend the NCCA meet in Austin, Texas. He also knew that most of them were thinking about him being in prison and the car accident. He was uncomfortable and had trouble concentrating on the sermon.

Trevor was a lot different in his style of preaching. He liked the way Coach had preached, but it seemed Trevor related more to the younger people. He used a lot more analogies, using everyday situations to present his message. He liked it.

This was also the first time he had been in this church when he was truly saved. Up to this point, he had just been listening to sermons that really didn't mean much to his life, but now that he was saved, he had a lot more interest in what was being said.

Boots was surprised after the service how many people came up and greeted him; it was almost as if they didn't know about prison.

The following morning after breakfast, Mrs. Turner said, "Let's go."

"Go where?" Boots asked.

"We are going to start your driving lessons," she said.

Boots was surprised that she was really serious about teaching him to drive. He thought she had said it the other day just to be nice.

Mrs. Turner had her own car, but she said they would take Bob's old car.

"It needs to be driven, and I'm sure Bob would want you to learn to drive in his car," she said.

Mrs. Turner drove out into the country where there wasn't much traffic. She got out of the car and walked around to the passenger side and told Boots to scoot over behind the wheel; the lesson had begun. This same procedure continued for the next month, until she thought he was ready to take his driving test. They had spent nights going over the written part of the test he would have to take.

The day Boots went to get his license, he was so nervous he felt like he used to before a big race. He passed and now could officially drive a car; he was only twenty-five years old.

He attended church service every Sunday and Wednesday night with Mrs. Turner.

He put several applications in for jobs but heard nothing. He even thought about going back and asking Mr. McCoy, but he knew nothing would have change; he was still a crook.

Trevor stopped by one afternoon to talk to Boots. He told Boots he wanted him to tell his life story at church services one Sunday.

Boots didn't think it would be a good idea. Plus, he would be so nervous he wasn't sure he could do it. Trevor spent the next several weeks convincing Boots that the story would be inspirational and show people that no matter how low and hopeless their situation in life seemed to be, if they trusted in God and believed in him, he could bring them out of the darkest situations.

"There is not a person in this church who has been a world champion and then was sent to prison. Your story will be a blessing and provide motivation to everyone in the church, no matter what their situation in life is," Trevor said.

It took several months of begging and pleading before Boots agreed to speak at the Wednesday-night service. Fewer people attended on

Wednesday night, and he wasn't sure he could talk in front of all the people at the Sunday service.

After presenting his story at the Wednesday-night service, the response was unbelievable. There was not a dry eye in the church. Everyone was shaking his hand and patting Boots on the back, saying how much the story had touched them.

After everyone had left and only Trevor, his family, and his mother were remaining, Trevor convinced Boots to repeat his story on Sunday. Boots wasn't sure he could speak before all those people, but he agreed.

The following Sunday, Trevor told the congregation that they were in for a special treat this morning. He went on to say, "Those of you who were here Wednesday night know what I'm saying is true.

"Mr. Harris, who we all know as Boots, is going to tell his amazing life story. Knowing his story, I have been trying to convince Boots to tell his story to the church for months. He finally agreed to tell it during the Wednesday-night service. I feel I'm not alone in saying I heard the story, but it is so fascinating that I could hear it over and over again.

"Without any more talk from me, let me introduce an Olympic champion and the New York Athletic Association Track Athlete of the Year for 1960, James Harris, or as we know him, Boots."

"Thank you, Pastor Turner, for that wonderful but misleading introduction. The kind pastor introduced me as an Olympic champion and New York Athletic Association Track Athlete of the Year, which I am. What he didn't say is I am also an ex-con who took an innocent person's life after drinking and getting behind the wheel of a car, with less than ten minutes of previous driving experience and no driver's license.

"You came here tonight because of the desire to see and hear an Olympic champion. I can tell you I am the most unworthy person in this room to tell people how to live. There is only one in this room tonight worthy of telling us how to live a happy and fruitful life, and that is our Savior, the Lord Jesus Christ.

"I reached the pinnacle as far as my athletic career goes, but I failed miserably as far as living the life I should have been living.

"One of my coaches, was also your pastor, kept telling me I needed to worry about my eternal life rather than the so-called riches in this life.

"It took killing an innocent elderly lady and going to prison to finally wake me up.

"People often try to make me feel better by saying it was an accident. It was no accident that I had been drinking that night. It was not an accident that I got behind the wheel of a car that I knew I had no business trying to drive. I chose to do all of those things.

"Because of me, an elderly lady's children don't get to see her anymore. Her grandchildren will never grow up knowing how grandmothers try to spoil them. Her husband of over fifty years now lives all alone, missing his sweet wife.

"It took all of this to happen before I woke up and realized what Pastor Turner had been telling me all of those years.

"I was like many of you in this room tonight. I was too concerned with making earthly riches and not eternal riches. Just when things seemed to be looking up financially, I blew it all by making some bad choices.

"I used to carry my Olympic gold medal with me everywhere I went. It was the most treasured thing I owned. Today I know it is just a piece of medal that will someday melt away. Like Coach Turner told me while in prison, someday we will be walking on streets of gold in heaven.

"So many of you in this room tonight would give anything to be an Olympic champion and have that gold around your neck, or some of you will probably buy gold for financial gains down the road, but what you need to be striving for is the gold that awaits us when we are heaven with the Lord.

"I have not even looked at the gold medal in months. It's lost its value and appeal for me. Instead of having it around my neck, I have a new goal, to walk on streets of gold someday, and I will because I asked God to forgive me of my sins and come into my life.

"If you don't know God as your personal Savior, don't do like I did and put it off until a tragedy wakes you up. We never know if we will make it home tonight before we die. The lady I killed that night thought she would make it home too, but she didn't. But the one good thing is people who knew and loved her knew she would be in heaven.

"I would like to thank you for taking the time tonight to come and listen to me. God loves you and wants you to be with him in heaven. I beg you tonight, if you don't know him as your personal Savior, do it before it is too late. Thank you."

The story of Boots's life went over even better than it had at the Wednesday-night service. People couldn't wait to tell Boots how much they appreciated and admired him; even the people who had heard the story on Wednesday night were thanking him again.

The last person to thank Boots was Mr. Barnes, his former employer. He told Boots what an inspirational story it was and handed him his business card. He asked him to call him the following day.

That night, Boots lay on his bed looking at the card. He didn't know what Mr. Barnes wanted to talk to him about, but he hoped it was a job of some kind. He had no money and was tired of sponging off of Mrs. Turner, so he decided to give Mr. Barnes a call the following day.

The next morning, he asked Mrs. Turner if he could use her phone. He called Mr. Barnes to see what he wanted of him.

After hearing Boots's story at the church service yesterday, he had contacted the pastor at his church and asked if they could have Boots present his story at his church; he was booked for the next Sunday.

Boots wasn't sure he could do it; it was one thing to talk to people who he knew but another to talk to strangers about his life.

Mr. Barnes reminded him of all the interviews he had done after the Olympics and New York Awards and told him just to pretend he was doing an interview.

Boots reluctantly accepted. He wasn't sure he could do this.

Mr. Barnes gave him the name and address of his church and told him what time to be there.

"Do you need a ride?" Mr. Barnes asked.

"I may," Boots said.

"Did you ever get your driver's license?" Barnes asked.

"I did, but I don't own a car," Boots replied.

"Call me the day before if you need a ride. Where are you working?" Mr. Barnes asked.

"Nowhere," Boots replied. "I have filled out a lot of job applications, but no one wants to hire an ex-con."

"You have a job," Barnes said. "It might be working in one of my fast-food kitchens, but I'll put you somewhere," he said.

Boots didn't know what to say—except thank you.

The following Sunday, Boots gave his life story at Mr. Barnes's church.

As he finished, an elderly man stood up in the back of the church and began to walk forward. Boots didn't know what was happening. He didn't know the man.

The man walked up to the pulpit where Boots was standing and said, "My wife is the one who was killed in the car accident. I am commanded by the Bible and the Lord to forgive. I want you to know that I forgive you for my wife's death. I know she is in heaven and forgives you too."

He reached over and hugged Boots. There was not a dry eye in the house. Boots couldn't even speak; he just kept hugging the man and sobbing.

This touching story made the local news and spread to the national news.

Area churches and clubs began having Boots speak and give his testimony. Many churches would give the call to come forward after his message, and hundreds came.

The following day, Boots was supposed to contact Mr. Barnes about which fast-food restaurant he would be working at. Mr. Barnes told him he would not have a job at a fast-food restaurant; he would have his old job back at the restaurant.

Later, a book was written about Boots's life. It became a best seller on the *New York Times* book list. The book became so popular that it was eventually made into a movie that received all kinds of awards.

Because of the success of the book and the movie, Boots made more money than he could ever imagine. He started an organization in Mississippi that supplied shoes to needed children all over the state. He also organized all kinds of track clubs for the less fortunate students in the state, and as a result, many of the students earned college scholarships to major universities. He still travels to the poor sections of Mississippi and tells his story to try to encourage kids to realize that they can make something of themselves no matter how poor their background is. He shows them the medal and tells them anything is possible if they just believe in themselves.

Boots also came through on a promise that he had made to himself years ago; he said if he ever became rich, he would go back and help the homeless shelter that took him in years ago. With the money he donated and was able to raise, the homeless shelter was enlarged to accommodate twice as many people as before. He also expanded the kitchen and made deals with food distributors to upgrade the amount and quality of the food served in the kitchen.

Boots also created several scholarships at the University of Tennessee for less fortunate students to be able to attend college; being an athlete was not a requirement to receive the scholarships.

Boots flew back to Mississippi to meet Mrs. Longhurst, who was now in her nineties, to thank her for all that she and Mr. Longhurst had done to help him and his parents. While there, he went out to the old shed where he had stored his parents' belongings and dug through the crates until he found those old boots that had started it so many years ago. He now takes those boots with him to sit on the podium when he is asked to tell his story. He has told his story over two hundred times now. He has to fly to many of his engagements. He now is able to sit near the window and look out without the stress he once had.

Today, Boots is happily married to the one and only girl he ever dated; they met while working at Mr. Barnes's restaurant, where she worked as a waitress.

Boots and his wife, Lindsey, have two young children, a boy and a girl. Boots has several of his awards, trophies, and pictures on display in his office at home. One day, his seven-year-old son asked his father why there was an old pair of boots in the middle of all those awards. Boots just laughed and told him those were what he wore when he started running track. Someday when he gets older, he will tell him the rest of the story.

After Mr. Barnes retired, he died a few years later, and Boots bought the restaurant. He kept the original name out of respect for his former boss.

Even though it is one of the most exclusive restaurants in town, each Thanksgiving and Christmas, it opens its doors to feed the homeless. They don't just get a low-cost meal; they are served turkey with all the trimmings on Thanksgiving, and on Christmas, they eat steak.

At Christmas, they are also given a little gift box containing the everyday necessities that they can never afford otherwise.

Boots sent George a letter telling him he owed his life to him and he had a job waiting for him when he got out. Boots held true to his word, and George has been working at Boots's restaurant for several years now. He also led George to Christ.

Boots still does speaking engagements occasionally, but now many are abroad, since most people in this country know the story of Boots.

Every time he gives his story, he is sad that it had to come at the expense of a person's life. He still has nightmares about the car accident so many years ago.

Boots had one more major thing to accomplish in his life, and it involved his children.

Boots's son, Richie, was approaching his sixteenth birthday in a few weeks. Boots told Richie to get in the car; they were going to take a little ride.

"Where are we going, Dad? You know I have a track meet later, don't you?"

"I'll have you back in time for the meet; don't worry," his dad said.

"So where are we going then?" Richie asked again.

"We are going to have your first driving lesson."

"Do you really mean it?"

"You're not going to wait until you are in your midtwenties like I did to learn to drive," Boots said.

"Do I get a car?" Richie asked excitedly.

"Hold your horses here; we are just learning to drive. You're not old enough to have a car yet."

"But if I had a car, you wouldn't have to come and pick me up after practices every day," Richie pleaded.

"No more car talk today; we are here for you to learn how to drive."

Boots slowed down and pulled into a cemetery. He parked the car and told Richie to get behind the wheel.

"What are we doing in a cemetery?" Richie asked. "There is nothing here but dead people."

"There is also a lot of paved road here with no cars to worry about. We can practice all kinds of maneuvers here without you having to worry about hitting another car."

After about an hour of instruction and practice, Boots told his son to turn into a small paved road and turn off the ignition.

"What are we stopping here for? I've got to get to the track meet."

"We've got plenty of time to make the meet," his father said. "Follow me. I want to show you something."

Richie followed his father up the hill to a gravestone.

His father stopped in front of the headstone and stared at it.

Richie read the names on the stone to himself—Ralph and Sue Jameson. Richie had never heard these names before. Maybe they were relatives?

To break the silence, Richie finally asked his dad who they were.

"This is the woman I killed when I was drinking and driving," his father replied.

Richie knew the story behind the accident his father was involved in many years ago, but he had never heard his father mention it before.

Richie didn't know what to say; he could see tears in his dad's eyes.

"Because of me, this fine woman lost her life. See the flowers on her grave? Probably her children or grandchildren put them there. Her children lost their mother because of me. Her grandchildren were not old enough to remember much about their grandmother. She had great-grandchildren she never got to meet. Her husband lived the latter years at home alone, before he was put into a nursing home because he couldn't take care of himself.

"He told me he forgave me for what I had done, but that didn't help him living those last few years of his life all alone."

Richie just stood and listened to his father, not knowing what to say.

"I got behind the wheel of a car after I had been drinking. I didn't know how to drive, but I let some friends of mine at the time talk me into it. I didn't want to drive, but I didn't want to look weak in front of my buddies.

"You need to learn from my mistakes. You need to understand that getting behind the wheel of a car is a big responsibility and can not only ruin your life, but it can also ruin lots of other people's lives as well. There is not a day goes by that I don't relive that night and wish I had been strong enough to not let my friends talk me into something I didn't want to do.

"I can't change what happened that night, but hopefully you can learn from what I did and not make the same dumb mistake. Be big enough to tell your friends no if they want you to do something you know is not right."

Boots turned and started walking toward the car.

"We need to go; you have a track meet to get ready for."

Richie sat quietly on the way to the track meet, thinking over all that had gone on. He knew that his dad would trade the Olympic medal and all of his other athletic accomplishments if he could have that one night over again, but he couldn't. He vowed to himself he wouldn't make the same mistake and let peer pressure cause him to do things he knew weren't right.

As they got out of the car and walked toward the track, Richie thanked his father for taking him to the cemetery and telling him his story.

"You're right, Dad. I'm not old enough to have a car yet. I'm glad you are my father."

Boots put his arm on Richie's shoulder and told him he was glad he was his son too.

The track meet turned out to be Richie's worst performance of the year, but in his mind, it was a day he wouldn't trade for anything.

Two years later when it was almost time for Jennie to start driving, her father took her to the same cemetery, just like he had done with Richie.

14

Mr. McCoy's Auto Sales went out of business after he was arrested and put in prison for several shady deals he was involved in, as well as tax fraud. It seemed Mr. McCoy forgot to give the government their fair share.

The Olympic medal made Boots famous, but his real legacy will be how many people he led to Christ by telling his story. He tells people how lucky he was that God allowed him to live long enough to secure his place in heaven. His main theme is do not put it off like he did.

The Olympic medal was donated to the University of Tennessee and hangs in the trophy case today alongside the picture of Boots carrying his mother's and father's Tennessee shirts around the Olympic Stadium in Rome. Boots was also inducted into the University of Tennessee's Hall of Fame. A special half-time presentation was conducted at a University of Tennessee basketball game. Boots, along with the other two inductees, was asked to say a few words, but Boots declined and just waved to the crowd; he still felt his life was a failure because of the woman's death.

Boots finally took the two classes he lacked and graduated from the University of Tennessee at the age of thirty-seven. As he was handed his diploma, he was asked to say a few words. He told the graduates and people attending the graduation that the diploma he had just received meant more to him than the gold medal he had won in the Olympic Games.

When people look in the trophy case at the University of Tennessee and see the picture and Olympic gold medal, very few know the story of Boots and the car accident. The book and movie about his life were so long ago, hardly anyone alive today even knows they exist. They look at his picture holding his parents' Tennessee shirts and know he must have been a great man. They don't know how his life changed for the worst that one horrible night.

Boots died at the age of eighty-eight as the result of a heart attack. There were hundreds of people at his funeral, most knowing the real story of his life.

Richie asked if he could speak about his father at the funeral.

Richie began by saying, "Even though many people came forward and gave their lives to Christ over the years after hearing my father's amazing story, he kept reliving the one life that was lost because of him. He could never forgive himself for what happened that night.

"The Bible says we will not remember the bad times here on earth. My father, on the other hand, could not rejoice in his unbelievable accomplishments in the athletic world and later on in business because of one mistake he made on a tragic night so many years ago. It haunted him for the rest of his life. Now that he is in heaven, I'm sure God will have Mrs. Jameson and my father meet and be good friends. The burden will finally be lifted from my father, and he will at last be at peace with himself.

"If you don't know the Lord as your personal Savior, I beg you to study the Bible and its prophecies, which prove that it is true. If you do come to know the Lord and die before I do, tell my father I'll meet him someday soon. When you get there, the celebration will make winning the Olympic gold medal look insignificant. God and angels will be cheering for you, not sinful man. God bless you."

Printed in the United States
By Bookmasters